OPERATOR #5:
PATRIOTS' DEATH BATTALION

SECRET SERVICE OPERATOR #5 ™

AMERICA'S UNDERCOVER ACE

PATRIOTS' DEATH BATTALION

By Curtis Steele

STEEGER BOOKS • 2021

CHAPTER 1
SURRENDER!

T HE HIGH droning buzz of a flight of enemy pursuit planes startled the two men in the dugout into swift attention. One of them, a young man, thin-faced, sharp-featured, wore the uniform of a lieutenant of infantry. The other was a grizzled, blue-jowled top sergeant. They both shaded their eyes, peering eastward into the rising sun. The black shapes winging swiftly toward them were strung out over the Mississippi—a full dozen of them, not flying in orderly formation, but seeming to race with each other. Behind the dugout, perhaps a quarter of a mile, were the hastily excavated trenches of the American Defense Force, which had been pushed back to the west bank of the Mississippi by the inexorable advance of the invading, goose-stepping troops of the mad emperor, Rudolph I, absolute master of the Central Empire, and now master by conquest of all that portion of the United States east of the Mississippi River.

And the insignia on the wings of those hurtling planes were easily distinguishable now—the severed head and the crossed broadswords—the banner under which Rudolph's father, Maximilian, had carried conquest and atrocity to Europe and Asia, and under which Canada and the eastern United States had been crushed.

The young lieutenant shuddered a little as he saw that dreadful insignia on the wings. He reached for the earphones at his

1

elbow, adjusted them hastily. He spoke hoarsely into the transmitter connecting him with the anti-aircraft battery in the trenches behind.

"Lieutenant Bledsoe talking, Observation Post Number One. It's an enemy squadron, sir. Give it—"

He stopped as the grizzled sergeant seized his elbow. "No, no, lieutenant. Tell the major to hold his fire. That first plane—look.

2

The mechanized armies of Rudolph were leaving death and destruction as far west as the Mississippi.

There's a man and a woman in it. And they're being chased by the others!"

Bledsoe exclaimed into the phone: "Hold it, Major!" He shaded his eyes, looked up. The leading plane was banking steeply upward. In the forward cockpit he could plainly see the streaming hair of a girl, reflecting darkly golden light from the glinting rays of the sun. In the rear cockpit was the thin shape of a smallish man. The man was leaning over the side, as if inspecting the terrain below.

Behind them the pursuing squadron fanned out, rising swiftly after them. Flame-colored tracer bullets streaked out at the fleeing plane from the machine guns of the Central Empire ships.

The lieutenant said: "Damn! It's the girl who's flying that crate. My God, she hasn't got a chance. They're right on top of her!"

The girl had leveled off, but instead of flying across the American lines she sped almost directly over the dugout, southward. The enemy pursuits were close on her tail, and the drumming of their machine guns was distinctly audible to the lieutenant and the sergeant above the hum of the motors. The fleeing plane had the same insignia as the others, and Lieutenant Bledsoe peered up, puzzled.

"You think it could be a trick of some kind, Geffen?" he asked the sergeant.

"I don't know, sir. I guess she can't land. Those buzzards would come down on top of her and shoot her to pieces while she was makin' a landing. Look, she's circling. And she's doin' some damn good flying, sir." There was admiration in the sergeant's voice as the girl threw her plane into a deep spin that just took her out of the path of a sizzling lane of slugs from the chattering guns behind her. She came out of the spin, climbed desperately, and circled back toward the dugout.

Lieutenant Bledsoe spoke into the telephone. "That plane that's stunting, sir. It has a girl and a man that seem to be trying to get away from the others. Do you think you could take a chance on popping a couple of shells at the others without hitting her? What? You can't? Too risky, eh? All right, sir. We'll have to wait."

Once more he stopped talking as the fleeing planes passed directly overhead. He uttered a gasp of amazement. For a slim shape had swung out of the rear cockpit, and was coming hurtling down toward them. It was the thin form of the little man. He dropped like a plummet, as the girl's plane screamed past, high above. Both the sergeant and Lieutenant Bledsoe watched that slim hurtling shape, while the pursuing squadron roared on. They watched, open-mouthed, saw a parachute billow open, saw the man's fall suddenly checked.

And they both shouted aloud in an agony of apprehension as they saw two of the enemy crates dip suddenly, come around in a wide, screaming back, and open up with machine guns upon the man dangling from the parachute.

"Good Lord!" Bledsoe groaned. "They can't do that! Why don't they give him a sporting chance?"

SERGEANT GEFFEN stood up in the dugout, his big hands clenched at his side, and threw hoarse curses up at those two murderous planes. He raised his clenched fists and shook them in the air, standing exposed, disregarding the hail of slugs that missed the descending man on the shoot and whined down all about him. "You damn murderers!" he shrieked. "Let be! Give him a break!"

The two planes shrieked down past the man in the air, climbed, and turned for another try. They hadn't got him that first try, because they hadn't gauged his descent accurately. They had been too sure of themselves. Now they were going to try again.

The man on the chute was manipulating the cords, coming down at a slant which would land him within a few yards of the dugout, calmly ignoring the threat of those two spitting machine guns. From the ground, Bledsoe and Geffen could see the helmeted pilots slipping into a steep power dive that would bring them down point blank at the dangling man.

Bledsoe gazed upward, fascinated. He groaned: "God, they've got him now, for sure!"

Suddenly, Sergeant Geffen opened his mouth and yelled at the top of his lungs: "Yeah, girl! Give 'em hell!"

He shook Bledsoe by the shoulder, forgetting the other's superior rank, shouting uncontrollably and pointing up to the south at the girl's plane. She had led her pursuers around in a wide circle, and now she was coming back, the wind screaming in her struts, her own machine-guns hammering out death at the two planes which were attacking the man on the chute. Behind her, the rest of the pursuing squadron were strung out in a long line, their machine guns silent. They didn't dare to fire now, for the girl was in a line with the two planes she was attacking. She was coming in at an angle, so her own tracers did not endanger the dangling man. But they were disastrous for the two enemy planes. One of them burst out into flames and the other fell into a tail spin that sent it down, past the man on the chute, to crash not a hundred feet from the dugout in which Bledsoe and Geffen stood. She continued in her dive, slipped past the man she had just saved, waved from the cockpit, and pulled out of her dive almost scraping the ground with her landing gear.

The plane she had set afire wavered dizzily, turned slowly and headed east, leaving a long plume of flame in its wake. Suddenly it broke its flight, plunged toward the earth, was lost in the muggy waters of the Mississippi. The plane that had crashed burst into flame also, and a staggering pilot scrambled out, ran a few feet, then stumbled and lay inert.

The man hanging from the chute had guided himself down to the ground now, and the leader of the enemy planes left off chasing the girl, swung and dived toward him. The man was struggling to untangle himself from the web of the chute, and was having difficulty.

Geffen shouted: "Hell, he can't get outta that. Here—" He stooped swiftly, raised a sub-machine gun from the floor of the dugout, brought it to his shoulder, sent a burst out at the diving enemy plane. The plane was too far, though, and Geffen's slugs spent themselves in the air. He cursed, threw another clip into the gun, and started to climb out of the dugout.

Bledsoe tried to stop him, but Geffen shook him off. "That guy's got guts!" he said. "We can't leave him there to be sprayed!" He started to run toward the struggling man, but stopped in

The enemy pilot banked sharply, barely escaping the girl's mad dive.

his tracks, looking upward with a flicker of admiration in his homely, rugged face.

A screaming, whining torpedo of death was hurtling down at that enemy plane. It was the ship flown by the girl. She wasn't shooting, she was just flying, in a relentless power dive pointed at a spot where it was inevitable that she and the enemy pilot should crash if neither swerved. The enemy pilot glanced quickly to his left, saw her coming, but kept on diving toward the man tangled in the chute. He didn't believe that the girl really meant to crash him.

Geffen was halted in his tracks, his lips moving. "You fool!" he was saying. "She'll do it! She'll crash you!"

It all happened in a second. They were both so close to the ground that Geffen could see the grim, merciless set of the enemy pilot's mouth. The roaring drone of the motor almost deafening him, mingling as it did with that of the girl's screaming plane. Geffen could see the girl, leaning down on her control stick, could see her face plainly, with her hair streaming out behind her. He knew why she didn't shoot. Her slugs, going past that enemy plane, would certainly strike the man entangled in the parachute cords. She was going to crash the other plane, rather than take a chance on hitting that man.

And the enemy pilot was the one to weaken! He fired a single burst down at the ground. It went wide, and he did not fire another. For he suddenly banked sharply to the left, skidded around on his left wing, barely in time to avoid the girl's sizzling plunge. She swept past the spot where he had been, pulled herself out of her dive, and veered around.

THE ENEMY pilot was still flying low, fighting to pull his plane out of the sharp turn he had taken. And Geffen suddenly grinned, shouted: "Oh, boy!" and raised his machine gun. He emptied the drum, and saw the pilot's head practically disintegrate under the hail of slugs he poured upward. The enemy plane wobbled, whirled into a dive, and struck the ground nose first, buckled over itself. It lay, a twisted heap of wreckage, from which flames suddenly sprang.

The rest of the enemy flight had hovered high above, watching their leader go down to settle the hash of the man who had landed. Now, seeing their leader downed, they moved into formation, and began a whizzing dive toward Geffen and the man in the chute. But the girl had risen high, flying to the south. The enemy flight was alone in the sky, and there was danger of hitting the girl. Apparently the major in charge of the anti-aircraft battery had been watching closely, for he seized his opportunity.

His guns, almost a quarter of a mile back, began to bark. Geffen started to dance with joy as the first shell struck the foremost enemy plane. There was a bright curtain of flame, a shrill explosion, and that first plane literally fell apart. A second and a third disappeared in a holocaust of fire and smoke. And the others quit. They turned tail and fled, leaving the girl in her crate, high in the air, and the man on the ground staggering to his feet out of the mass of cordage from the parachute. He had worked methodically, unhurriedly, as if trusting to the gods to protect him, and he had at last managed to get himself free.

He stood on the ground, with the flaming wreckage of an

enemy plane not fifty feet from him, and waved up to the girl in the plane above. From far up there a white hand fluttered, and the girl's plane winged its way eastward after the disappearing enemy flight.

Geffen stared up unbelievingly. "Holy mackerel!" he muttered. "After dropping this guy, and giving those birds hell, she's going back there! If they lay hands on her, they'll crucify her, sure as shootin'!"

He shook his head, dropped the machine gun, and ran toward the man who had climbed free of the chute. He met him halfway, stopped and stared in astonishment. His grizzled old face wore a ludicrous expression. He put his hands on his hips, stared at the slim figure of the person who had dropped in the parachute in defiance of the guns of a whole squadron of enemy pursuit planes. "My God," he demanded, "whose kid are you? Does your pa know you're stayin' out after bedtime?"

The person whom he faced was a freckle-faced lad of not more than fifteen, with a pert Irish nose and quick, intelligent eyes. He looked up at Geffen and smiled. When he smiled his whole face seemed to be illuminated. "Thanks, sarge," he said, "for shooting that bird down with the machine gun. He would have got me in another minute."

"Hell," said Geffen, "that wasn't me. It was the dame up there that saved you. She dived for the guy, and he didn't have the guts to stick. But listen, how does a kid like you come to be mixed up in this here war? What's your name?"

"My name," the boy said simply, "is Timothy Donovan. I've got important information. I'd like to be taken to headquarters at once. Rudolph is planning a big push for ten o'clock this morning. If we're not ready for it, our name will be mud!"

Geffen gaped at him. "I've heard of you. You're the kid that always goes around with Operator 5.* Orders came through

---

* AUTHOR'S NOTE: Regular readers of these chronicles will at once have recognized Tim Donovan and his freckle-faced, snub-nosed Irish lad who has been Operator 5's constant companion through many of his amazing exploits. Three years ago, on the lower east side of New York, Operator 5 has stepped into the shadow of death. And a hungry, shivering little boot-black had saved him from assassination. Ever since then the two have been almost inseparable. And Tim Donovan had more than once since that time proved himself an invaluable assistant, resourceful, courageous, worshiping the ground upon which Operator 5 trod. Too young to be admitted officially to the ranks of Intelligence, he has served as Operator 5's unofficial assistant, being privileged to be one of the handful of mortals to share the secret of Operator 5's true identity. When Operator 5, as a last resource, was made chief-of-staff of the American Defense Forces in an effort to stop the ruthless invasion of the Central Empire under the merciless Rudolph I, Tim Donovan had volunteered to undertake the work of Operator 5 behind the enemy lines while his hero took active command of the field forces. With great misgivings Operator 5 had allowed him to go. Tim had been captured, as he intimates to Geffen, and aided to escape by the young lady whom we

yesterday to keep on the lookout for you. There was a rumor you were captured."

"I was," the boy told him soberly. "But for the love of Pete, let's get out of the open. When those crates come back and report that I got away, Rudolph will probably lay down a barrage on this sector that will make your remember your prayers!"

GEFFEN GRINNED. "All right, kid. Come on. But who was that spunky dame? And what was the idea of her going back? They'll probably chop her head off. That's Rudolph's pet entertainment."

They were moving quickly toward the dugout, where Lieutenant Bledsoe was awaiting him.

"That girl," said Tim Donovan, "helped me to escape. I was slated for the ax this morning, but she got me out of the hoosegow and borrowed one of Rudolph's planes. She's Rudolph's cousin, and he wouldn't dare behead her. But"—Tim shuddered—"I'd feel better if she'd come across the lines with me!"

At the dugout, he swiftly introduced himself to Lieutenant Bledsoe, who phoned back to headquarters. The lieutenant looked toward the east anxiously while he held the phone, waiting for his connection. He shook his head. "If we had any planes left," he said, "those crates wouldn't have got away. But here we are, without a decent air force, with our big guns silent because of lack of ammunition, and trying to hold a two thousand mile front against the most experienced and best trained army that

have seen so far only in the air, but whom we shall be privileged to meet more closely and more intimately as this story progresses.

the world has ever seen! Son, I doubt if even your friend, Operator 5, can save the country from complete conquest!" *

---

* AUTHOR'S NOTE: The situation at this time was indeed precarious for the American Defense Force. Sixty days ago, the troops of the Central Empire had completed their conquest of Canada, and had marched into New England. Their then-emperor, Maximilian I, was ambitious, merciless—and a brilliant general. From the position of Dictator of the military European country of Balkaria he had made war upon the rest of Europe, just as Napoleon Bonaparte had done a hundred and thirty years ago. But he had not yet met with a Waterloo. One after another the nations of Europe yielded to the yoke of Maximilian. Then had followed a great part of Asia. And Maximilian, now crowned as Emperor of Europe and Asia, had cast his eyes upon America. With the combined armies and navies of Europe and Asia under his command, he sailed across the seas, quickly subdued Canada, and led his conquering, goose-stepping cohorts into the United States. We were totally unprepared for the avalanche. Many had prated of our natural strength, of the bulwarks which the Atlantic and Pacific Oceans constituted. Funds had been stinted for national defense. Our guns, our planes, our chemical warfare branches were hopelessly outclassed and outmoded by the supremely developed militarism of the Central Empire. In sixty days the country east of the Mississippi from the Great Lakes to the Gulf of Mexico was in the hands of the Central Empire. And what constituted a greater cataclysm, Maximilian had been assassinated, and his son, Rudolph, had become emperor. Rudolph possessed none of the great qualities of his father, and all of his inhuman ones—plus a good deal. It was Rudolph who had devised the devilish plan of marching hundreds of thousands of chained captives alongside of his regular troops, so that whenever an American barrage was laid down the gunners

Lieutenant Bledsoe's eyes were bloodshot from lack of sleep. His thin, sharp face was drawn with weariness and worry. Like every other officer and private in the American Defense Forces, he had long ago given up hope of driving the troops of Rudolph out of the country. They were even despairing of being able to check the Central Empire's march to the Pacific Ocean and complete conquest.

Diane

Tim Donovan exclaimed enthusiastically: "Listen, lieutenant, don't be a wet blanket. You don't know Operator 5 the way I do. He's never failed at anything he ever undertook. This is a big job—the biggest he ever tried—but I'll bet my shirt on him!"

Bledsoe eyed him enviously, sighed. "It's good to be young, and to have such faith! If what you say were only true!" Bledsoe was not so much older than Tim, but sixty days of the horror of this invasion had aged him cruelly. He was about to say more when his connection was established. He reported to corps headquarters that Tim Donovan was there, held the line while corps headquarters called staff headquarters in Kansas City.

Tim Donovan said anxiously: "I want to talk to Operator 5 personally. I heard Rudolph and his generals planning the big push for ten o'clock this morning. They're going to open a

would know that they were massacring their own countrymen. And this sadist was steadily marching toward the Pacific!

15

blanket bombardment at five minutes to ten, all along the front. And while we're occupied with that, they're going to launch a fleet of boats from the east shore of Lake Superior, and from Canada, and come down on Duluth like a ton of bricks. Then they'll march south in a flanking movement, and take us from behind! I've got to warn Operator 5! If Rudolph gets a foothold in Minnesota he can cut off our lines of communication, and starve us to surrender!" *

* AUTHOR'S NOTE: In order to gain a better idea of the full import of Tim Donovan's news, a brief recapitulation of the military position may be helpful. To date, the American forces had suffered five overwhelming defeats. At the beginning of the invasion, the Central Empire had made use of a new and potent gas, known as the Green Gas, which was capable of spreading over great areas and destroying all life within those areas. The gas was used in Maine, and later in the southeastern section of the United States. Four million American soldiers and non-combatants had perished by the Green Gas before Operator 5, working independently, was able to destroy the formula for the deadly chemical. There was now no longer any fear of the Green Gas. But Rudolph had a foothold in the United States. And more than that, he had so disrupted American defense that the resistance which his goose-stepping troops met was negligible. The great armament and steel plants of the country were at once pressed into service to turn out guns and ammunition and planes with which to meet the avalanche of conquest. But Rudolph had planes and guns and ammunition already manufactured. He knew where our plants were, and he had the tools with which to destroy them. In four days he destroyed the great cities where our large plants were located. His troops pushed on, southward and westward, irresistibly. Our air

Bledsoe exclaimed: "Good Lord, son, we better report this at once!" He jiggled the hook of the phone impatiently, and in a moment was talking to Kansas City. He spoke into the mouth-piece jerkily: "We have the young man, Tim Donovan, here. He just flew over the lines, escaping from the Central Empire troops. He has vital information. Can you let him talk to Operator 5 at once? What's that? All right, I'll hold it."

HE FROWNED, turned his head toward Tim. "They say Operator 5 isn't there. General Redfern will talk to you."

Tim's freckled face flushed. "What! That big stuffed shirt? Where's Operator 5?"

It was General Redfern who had been superseded in command by Operator 5 at the order of the President. Tim said: "Gee, Redfern is the one man I *don't* want to talk to. He hates—"

---

force, as Bledsoe pointed out, was annihilated in the first week of combat. We ran short of ammunition for our big guns. The situation was well-nigh hopeless when Operator 5 was appointed Chief of Staff by the President. And the first thing Operator 5 did was to steal a leaf from the book of the Russians. When Napoleon marched into Russia, the Muscovites retreated to the west shore of the Mississippi along a twenty-five hundred mile front. He had insisted on the evacuation of Duluth, Saint Paul, Saint Louis, Memphis, New Orleans, and every other city and town along the great river. Now there was not a single non-combatant in those cities except those engaged in supplying the armed forces. The American Defense Force was dug in along the river, ready to meet the shock of the first attack of the Central Empire. But if Duluth were taken, the whole line of defense would be endangered. The news was of utmost importance.

He stopped as Bledsoe spoke into the transmitter: "Just a moment, sir. Here's Tim Donovan." The lieutenant pulled the earphones from his own head, handed them to Tim. "Better talk to him anyway, son. This is war. You got to do a lot of things you don't like—in war."

Tim shrugged, donned the earphones. "General Redfern? This is Tim Donovan. I—"

Redfern's cold, precise voice came to him over the wire. "What do you want, boy? Be quick. I have little time to waste—"

Tim Donovan broke in. "All right, sir, don't waste it. Just let me talk to Operator 5."

"Operator 5 isn't here. If you have information, give it to me, quickly. I am in temporary command. I hear you learned something of importance inside the enemy lines."

"But where is Operator 5?" Tim persisted.

Redfern barked: "I am in command, I tell you. Never mind where that young fool is. Give me your report, or I will have you placed under arrest and brought here!"

Tim glanced helplessly at Bledsoe, who had been able to hear every word of the conversation because of the general's foghorn voice.

"Go on, son," Bledsoe urged. "Tell him. There's little time."

Jimmy Christopher

Tim shrugged, nodded, and spoke into the phone. "Very well, sir. I have to report that the Central Empire is planning an attack all along the front for ten o'clock this morning."

"That is no news," Redfern interrupted coldly. "We already know that."

"Wait, sir," Tim rushed on eagerly. "That attack is only a

cover for their real intentions. They're going to make a flank movement against Duluth by water across Lake Superior, and by land from Canada. That'll bring them down behind our line along the Mississippi, and they'll cut off our communications."

Redfern's laugh brought the lad up short. "Thanks for nothing, boy. Like the rest of Operator 5's associates, your information is worthless. There will be no big attack at ten o'clock."

"But I tell you, sir, it's so. I heard it."

"And there will be no flank movement against Duluth. We are about to sign an armistice with the Central Empire. Acting upon the advice of myself and the General Staff, the President is throwing himself and the country on the mercy of Emperor Rudolph. We can no longer continue our resistance. In an hour, if the armistice is signed, the signal will go out to cease hostilities!"

Tim Donovan's voice broke with urgent anxiety. "Good God, General Redfern, you can't do that! We can still put up a fight. You don't know this Rudolph. You should have seen the things I saw in the conquered territory—"

The lad stopped talking, and his shoulders sagged. He was speaking into a dead line. General Redfern had hung up on him. He glanced up to see Sergeant Geffen and Lieutenant Bledsoe looking at him queerly. "You—heard?" he asked almost in a whisper.

Geffen's lips were twitching. Bledsoe said in a whisper: "They're selling us out! They're throwing in the sponge!"

Tim Donovan's little fists clenched spasmodically. "We mustn't let them do it! Rudolph is a madman. He delights in torture and pain. He'll crucify the rest of the country, the way he's been doing in the conquered territory. God, what's come over the General Staff? We've got to stop them!"

Bledsoe put a hand on the boy's shoulder. "How can we stop them, son? We're nobody. But where is your friend, Operator 5? How come Redfern is suddenly back in command? Can anything have happened to Operator 5?"

Suddenly Tim clutched Bledsoe's arm. "Lieutenant! There's something radically wrong in Kansas City. I want to go there. I've got to find out what's happened to Jimmy Christopher. Can you get me some sort of transportation?"

Bledsoe shook his head. "You'd have to talk to the commanding officer of the sector. I have no authority."

"But I can't waste time. Redfern said they'd sign the armistice in an hour. Please—"

BLEDSOE GLANCED across Tim's shoulder at Sergeant Geffen. The two men looked at the boy appraisingly. "I'm sure every man in the line would rather die right here than see their wives and daughters become slaves of Rudolph. But we can't do anything about it. If our leaders give up, how can we fight? And even if we got you to Kansas City, what could you do?"

"I could find Jimmy Christopher—Operator 5!" Tim told them eagerly. "I'm sure he never consented to this. They must have done something to him, or he'd never let it go through. And maybe he needs help!"

Once more Bledsoe and Geffen glanced at each other. Geffen said slowly: "The kid deserves a chance, Lieutenant. He's got spunk—" the sergeant put a big paw on the boy's shoulder, squeezed affectionately—"and if he's got such faith in this Operator 5, then Operator 5 must have the goods. Let's give the kid his chance. Why should we hang out in this lousy dugout when the General Staff's selling us out?"

Bledsoe said thoughtfully: "You mean—we'd go with the boy?"

Geffen nodded. "Sure. We'd be guilty of deserting our post, but what the hell? If we're stood up against a wall and shot, it won't be any worse than kissing Rudolph's feet and taking an oath of allegiance to the dirty maniac!"

"All right!" Bledsoe exclaimed abruptly. "We'll do it! Come on, kid!" He waved to Geffen. "Get the bathtub ready, sergeant!"

There was a suspicious moisture in Tim's eyes. "You're… really coming with me… to Kansas City?"

Geffen was already in a corner of the dugout, wheeling out a motorcycle with side-car attached. It was a front line messenger's motorcycle with which all observation posts were equipped in the event that the field telephone should be put out of commission.

Bledsoe's eyes were shining. "Right, kid! We're going with you! We'll see if we can find your friend—and we'll also see what's got into this General Staff of ours. And if we're shot for trying, to hell with us!"

"Attaboy!" Sergeant Geffen roared. He seized the telephone cord, gave it a terrific yank, and pulled it out. He grinned at Tim Donovan. "I've been thinkin' about doing that for two days. Now I feel better!"

CHAPTER 2
ON THE TRAIL OF
THE TRAITOR

COUNT LEOPOLD VON HAUGLEIN carelessly flicked the ash from his fat cigar on to the floor. He arose and drew down the tunic of his brilliantly decorated uniform—that of a staff major in the Expeditionary Forces of the Central Empire. He waved his hand at the others in the room. "Those, gentlemen, are the only terms upon which His Imperial Majesty, Rudolph I, will grant you an armistice. Take them or leave them!"

He showed his white teeth in a suave smile, turned his back on the other occupants of the room, and stood looking out of the window at the pulsing life in the City Hall square of Kansas City, where ragged, hastily recruited American troops were being made ready to march to the front line trenches.

Behind him, the four men to whom he had delivered his ultimatum glanced at each other unhappily. The President of the United States sat at a broad desk near the opposite window. Standing about him were Brigadier-General Redfern, Admiral Sinnott, and Colonel Hartley. The President, who had been fifty-two years old at his inauguration, two years ago, now looked seventy. His shoulders sagged from fatigue and sleeplessness, and deep lines were etched in his cheeks. Black hollows shone under his eyes. He looked down at the sheet of paper on his desk, then looked up at the brightly uniformed back of the emissary from the Central Empire. No man was ever permitted to turn

23

his back on the President of the United States; and this studiedly insolent gesture was an indication of the manner in which Rudolph and his counselors intended to treat those whom they conquered.

The President spoke in a hollow, beaten voice. "But these terms, Count von Hauglein—" he tapped the sheet of paper on the desk—"are not the terms of an armistice; they are terms of abject surrender. You demand that our men lay down their arms and evacuate the trenches along the entire front; you require that I and my Chief of Staff immediately go with you to the headquarters of Emperor Rudolph and place ourselves subject to his order. That is not armistice, Count von Hauglein. That is surrender!"

Hauglein swung away from the window. He was no longer smiling. "Yes, Mr. President, it is surrender. And why should it be otherwise? You are beaten. Beaten, you understand?" He waved his hand toward the window. "You are recruiting fifteen-year-old youths to fill your trenches. We have decimated your armies, destroyed your fleet. Your air force was annihilated weeks ago. Our guns outrange yours by fifty percent. We have destroyed your ordnance and ammunition plants. You have nothing to fight with. You must bend the knee, or be entirely destroyed. Our emperor, Rudolph, would be just as glad if you did not yield. He hates your country, and he would welcome the opportunity to visit the western portion with the same destruction that he has visited upon the eastern section! It was only with the greatest difficulty that we persuaded him to grant you this chance to escape further punishment." Von Hauglein shrugged. "The choice is yours, Mr. President!"

The President said hoarsely: "But you offer us no guarantees of safety for our citizens—for our women and children. Rudolph has been ruthless in the East. At least promise us that he will be more merciful from now on."

Von Hauglein smiled thinly. "No promises. No one can predict what our emperor will think of next. He may order a million of you beheaded; or he may send your women and children into the mines and factories as he has done in the East; or he may suddenly decide to exercise clemency. You must take your chances. But decide quickly!" The President rested his elbows on the desk, buried his head in his hands. He groaned: "If only Operator 5 had not disappeared like this. He had the courage to go on fighting against any odds."

Von Hauglein laughed shortly. "You are fortunate that Operator 5 is not here. That young fool would go on fighting, and our emperor would then destroy every living being in your country. It is a good thing for you that General Redfern here is experienced enough to know when he is beaten." He glanced at his wrist watch. "You must decide quickly. My master awaits your answer. If it should be in the negative, he is prepared to launch an offensive that will shatter your line like glass!"

The President gazed helplessly at Redfern, Sinnott and Hartley. "Gentlemen," he said, "what do you advise?"

Sinnott and Hartley shrugged. "The decision," Sinnott told the president, "is up to General Redfern. In the absence of Operator 5, he knows more about our chances than anybody else."

REDFERN SAID explosively: "I've advocated making peace with the Central Empire for the past week. We have no possible chance of withstanding a determined advance by Rudolph's troops. At Operator 5's orders, all the Mississippi bridges but one have been blown up. But that won't stop the Central Empire. Their big guns can blast us out of the trenches along the Mississippi. They can drive us back for miles, and their engineers can throw pontoon bridges across. Besides, the river can be forded at many spots. Our losses in men have been devastating thus far; if we yield now, we will at least have the remnants of a nation left, even though we be subjugated to the Purple Emperor. I, for one, am convinced that the wiser course is to make peace. I am ready to take the oath of allegiance to Emperor Rudolph I. It is a bitter pill to swallow, but I don't want to see our country utterly destroyed!"

While Redfern was talking, his face had gone a deep red. He was himself a brave man. But he believed that it was impossible to continue the one-sided struggle any longer.

The President sighed. "So be it. Count von Hauglein, I will be ready within an hour to go with you. General Redfern has already notified the commanding officers at the front that we are negotiating an armistice. Will you notify your troops to cease hostilities?"

Von Hauglein bowed. "It shall be done. But please remember

that one of my master's demands is that your Chief-of-Staff also surrender to him."

The President nodded. "General Redfern will accompany me."

"Excuse me, Mr. President. Emperor Rudolph does not mean General Redfern. He means the man who was your Chief-of-Staff until last night—Operator 5. It is that man whom he wants above all else. He would give a kingdom to get him in his power. You *must* bring Operator 5!"

The President exclaimed bewilderedly: "But I don't know where Operator 5 is! He disappeared last night. If he were here, I am sure he would not consent to these terms. I cannot produce him!"

Von Hauglein shrugged. "That is too bad, Mr. President. All our negotiations must fall through unless Operator 5 accompanies you. You should surely be able to find him—he cannot disappear into thin air."

"But he may be dead. He may have been killed!"

"Very well, then produce his body. My master would prefer to have him alive. If he is dead, that will have to do. But alive or dead, he must be produced!"

Redfern glanced from Sinnott to Hartley, then took a step forward. "I think, Count von Hauglein, that I will be able to find Operator 5."

The President started, looked up sharply. "Redfern! You know where he is?"

"I said I thought I could produce him. You will be satisfied, Count von Hauglein, if he is dead?"

27

"Yes," said the Imperial emissary.

"Very well. Give us an hour." He bowed, and left the room, accompanied by Sinnott and Hartley, while the President followed them with narrowed, suddenly suspicious eyes. After they had left, von Hauglein said: "A good man, Redfern. He is sensible. My master may reward him by placing him in charge of the new local government to be set up."

The President slowly arose from behind his desk. His face was white, and there was a terrible pain in his eyes. His hand, shaking almost uncontrollably, drew the heavy service revolver from his holster. Von Hauglein, startled, took a half step forward, then stopped short. The President was saying in a dull voice: "I have lived to see my country thrown into chains; I have lived to see treachery among the highest in command; I have lived to see the decline and fall of the great American republic. I have lived too long. You said that you would take Operator 5, dead. Take me that way, too, Count von Hauglein!"

And before the uncomprehending Imperial emissary could stop him, the President of the United States of America raised the gun to his own temple, pressed the muzzle hard against the skin beneath the graying hair, and pulled the trigger.

The Chief Executive of the United States sprawled dead across the desk, with his brains blown out by his own hand, his blood staining a deep carmine the paper on which was written the peace ultimatum from Rudolph I, Emperor of the Central Empire, Lord of Europe and Asia, and conqueror of North America.

And Count Leopold von Hauglein did not move, but gazed

with cold eyes upon the still warm, pitiful body. "It is well," he murmured.

GENERAL REDFERN, Admiral Sinnott and Colonel Hartley did not hear the shot which ended the life of the President of the United States. They were already outside of the City Hall Building. They stood for a moment in the hot sunlight, watching the dusty, weary youths marching past to entrain for the front lines. General Redfern motioned to a staff orderly who had been waiting in the corridor and who had followed them out. "My compliments to Colonel Huston," he said. "Tell him to suspend all further troop movements to the front. We are about to sign an armistice with the Central Empire."

The orderly saluted and left. A second orderly stepped up at Redfern's command, and to him the general said: "Communicate at once with General Judley at the front. Instruct him to begin evacuation of the front line trenches. Central Empire troops will begin occupation within an hour. No resistance is to be offered. We have agreed to terms of peace offered by Emperor Rudolph."

The orderly gazed at him, wide-eyed.

"Well," Redfern barked. "What are you gaping at?"

"Excuse me, sir. Did you say we are accepting their peace terms? We're surrendering?"

"Yes."

"But, sir, that's suicide. Look what they've done in the East—"

"Stop!" Redfern shouted. "Do you want to be court-martialed?"

"N-no, sir."

"Then carry out my instructions!"

29

The orderly saluted, backed away, with a queer, hopeless look in his eyes.

Redfern and his two companions did not move, but stood in silence for a long minute. Finally, Admiral Sinnott sighed and said: "Well, I suppose it was the only way." He repeated as if to himself: "The only way—to avoid utter destruction." He was a man of fifty, straight, slim, imposing in his dress uniform of a rear admiral of the United States Navy. But his head hung, and he did not raise his eyes from the ground.

"The only way," he repeated once more. "But just the same, I feel like a damned Judas!"

"Snap out of it, Sinnott!" Redfern barked. "Operator 5 was a menace to the country while he was in command. Suppose we bend the knee now. Our chance may come another time. Rudolph can't live forever. The Central Empire may break up— it's too unwieldy. Then we'll have our chance to throw off the yoke. But what chance would we have if we were all destroyed?"

Colonel Hartley nodded. "Redfern's right, Sinnott. We're buying a chance at revenge—and freedom."

"Yes," Admiral Sinnott said bitterly. "But at what a price! We preserve life, and lose honor, freedom, everything! Well, we're committed. Let's go!"

Redfern smiled, raised his hand and summoned a staff car. "Get out," he ordered the chauffeur. "I'll drive myself."

The three officers entered the car, and Redfern took the wheel, drove over toward the river front. None of them noticed the small Ford which had been parked at the far end of the square, and which swung in behind them, followed at a careful distance, keeping at such an angle that Redfern would not be apt to notice it through his rear vision mirror. This Ford was driven by a beautiful, chestnut-haired girl in the uniform of a field ambulance driver. Her softly modeled face was set in tight lines of anxiety, and her white, small teeth were biting into her lower lip. Her little hands were clenched hard around the rim of the wheel, and her eyes never left the staff car ahead.

Had Redfern or his two companions noticed that Ford, the whole course of world history might have been changed on that sunny morning in Kansas City.

Snuggled in the back seat of the Ford, huddled as far back as possible, sat a thin man of perhaps forty, with small, shrewd eyes. He had his hat off and was mopping his bald head with a handkerchief, held in long, supple fingers. He spoke urgently to the girl in the front seat.

"For God's sake, Miss Elliot, don't lose that car. I'll swear Redfern knows where Jimmy Christopher is. I heard him say he could produce Operator 5. That means he knows where he is, don't it?"

The girl kept her eyes on the staff car ahead, spoke over her shoulder. "I hope you're right, Slips. But how did you manage to overhear them?"

The man grinned. "Like I told you, Miss Elliot, I was in there snoopin' around to see could I find some clue to where Jimmy disappeared to. Well, I was poking around in Redfern's office, and there came steps out in the corridor. Someone was coming in, an' if I stayed they'd catch me. So I slipped out the side door, but I didn't go away. I stuck my ear to that door, and listened.

There was this von Hauglein, and the President, and them three in the car. I heard them give up, and I heard Redfern promise to produce Operator 5—alive or dead!"

The girl's lips trembled. "God grant he's alive!"

THESE TWO, in the Ford, were members of a small, intimate circle which alone knew the true identity of Operator 5—knew that he was Jimmy Christopher in private life. Diane Elliot, star reporter of the Amalgamated Press, loved Jimmy Christopher well enough to understand that his life was dedicated to the service of his country, and that marriage was not for him. She was content to wait, to share his adventures, and to find her happiness in the same dangerous paths which Operator 5 trod. It was she who had first kindled the spark of resistance in the people of the country in the early days of the Central Empire invasion, by refusing to take the oath of allegiance to the emperor. That refusal almost cost her pretty head.* When

---

* AUTHOR'S NOTE: Those of our readers who have read previous chronicles of the exploits of Jimmy Christopher—Operator 5 of the United States Intelligence—will recall that Diane Elliot has often, by her resourcefulness and courage, succeeded in undertakings assigned to her by Jimmy Christopher where a man might have failed. As mentioned above, in the early days of the Central Empire invasion, she had been in the Occupied Territory of New York when the goose-stepping troops of the Purple Emperor invested in the great metropolis and placed the iron heel of oppression upon the necks of non-combatants. She was sentenced to decapitation along with thousands of others who refused to take the oath of allegiance to the Purple Emperor. And it was only by a clever, dangerous ruse that Jimmy Christopher and

Operator 5 had taken over command of the organized resistance to the Central Empire, she had enlisted in the ambulance service, but had not yet left for the front when Jimmy Christopher disappeared.

The man, Slips McGuire, an ex-pickpocket, was one of the most devoted followers of Operator 5. It was Jimmy Christopher who had pulled him out of the morass of crime, had given him a chance to serve his country, and had awakened in him once more the self-respect without which no man can live a full life. On several occasions those long, supple fingers of Slips McGuire, ex-pickpocket, had helped Jimmy Christopher by using an unlawful skill for a lawful purpose.

Now they were following the one single clue to the whereabouts of their friend. And at the same time, the boy, Tim Donovan, was speeding westward in the sidecar of the military motorcycle, sitting on the broad lap of Sergeant Geffen, while Lieutenant Bledsoe, raw-faced from the hot wind, squeezed the last mile of speed out of the hot engine.

Diane Elliot. Tim Donovan. Slips McGuire. Three individuals all racing toward the same objective. Three individuals whose

Tim Donovan had saved her from the gleaming broadsword of the executioner. That brilliant rescue had not, however, stopped the bloody executions of others. And even now, in every conquered city in the United States, there were daily processions of tumbrels, making their creaking way to the chopping block, filled with men and women who refused to acknowledge the Purple Emperor as their lord and master.

singleness of purpose, whose devotion to a common friend and leader, were destined to change the march of history!

CHAPTER 3
THE MAN IN THE IRON MASK

THE MAN who lay on the cot stirred and opened his eyes. For a moment he lay absolutely quiet, letting his gaze wander over the four bare walls of the small cell. There was no window, but dim light filtering in from somewhere in the corridor showed him that there was nothing in the room but the cot upon which he was stretched.

He tried to move, and flinched. Sharp pain shot through his head. He tried to lift a hand, found that he couldn't. His arms felt numb. It was a full minute before he realized that they were tied behind his back. His feet, also, were tightly laced together at the ankles.

He sighed, let his head fall back on the hard bare wood of the cot. Fiery pains were shooting from the back of his head, flickering in darting flashes of agony in his eyes. But his face betrayed no fear, no consternation. It was a clean-cut face, youthful, with a firm mouth, a straight nose and a determined chin.

His body was naked from the waist up, revealing smooth, rippling muscles that bulged now as he exerted all his strength in an effort to burst the bonds that confined his wrists. He met with no success. Whoever had tied them had done a good job.

The prisoner raised his knees in the air, pushed with his bound hands and jerked himself into a sitting position, then swung his feet off the cot, let them rest on the floor. His head swam, and he leaned back, resting it against the wall. His eyes, glancing down at the cot, saw that the board was clotted with dark blood. His lips twisted into a bitter smile. The spot where that clotted blood defaced the board was the spot where his head had lain. He saw, too, that his shoulder

Slips McGuire

and upper right arm were discolored with congealed blood.

He started as the tread of footsteps became audible in the corridor. A cold, precise voice spoke: "You are sure he is not dead?"

Another voice answered: "No, General, he isn't dead. I looked in a little while ago. He was still unconscious, but he was breathing regularly. The man should have a doctor, but you specifically ordered that no one should come near him, so I didn't get one."

The precise voice replied: "That was right. No one must even suspect that he is a prisoner here. If the populace and the troops suspected it, there might be bloody riots."

The steps had come close to the grilled door. "This is his cell, General. There are no other prisoners in this wing. I kept him strictly separate, as you ordered."

A switch clicked outside, and brilliant light sprang from an overhead bulb, high up in the ceiling, protected by mesh wire. The light blinded the prisoner. He heard a key grate, heard metal sliding, and the door swung open. The cold voice said: "We three will go in. You may leave the door open, but retire to your office.

"... You will be the Man
in the Iron Mask!"

When we want you we will send for you. Remember, you must utter no word of what goes on here. I shall hold you strictly accountable for that."

The prisoner arose with an effort from the cot, steadied himself on his bound feet and faced the three men who filed solemnly into the cell. His lips were drawn into a tight, bitter line, and his eyes were bleak. He said mockingly: "How do you

do, General Redfern? How do you do, Admiral Sinnott? How do you do, Colonel Hartley? It is a pleasure to welcome three such *good* friends to my humble quarters. It is a pleasure to be visited by such *honorable* gentlemen!"

There was steel in his voice, and it seemed to cut like a lash at the three officers. Two of them—Hartley and Sinnott—lowered their eyes before the scorn in his glance. Redfern did not. The general's face reddened, and he carefully bent and placed upon the cot a package which he was carrying. Then he straightened, coughed, and said to the prisoner: "Operator 5, we don't care what you think of us. We are acting for what we consider the best interests of our country."

Jimmy Christopher—Operator 5 of the United States Intelligence—did not take his eyes from Redfern. "You brought me here by a ruse, the three of you. You waited till my back was turned; and then one of you—I guess it was you, Redfern—hit me on the head with an automatic. I was just succeeding in coördinating the defenses of the country against the Central Empire. What was your purpose in making me a prisoner here—if not to betray the country?"

Admiral Sinnott clenched his hands. "Damn you, Operator 5, don't call us traitors. We felt that with you in command, the people would never consent to making peace on Rudolph's terms. And if we were to continue to fight for another week, Rudolph would annihilate us. We have no guns, no planes, no ammunition. Yet you wanted to continue the hopeless resistance. Rather than see the country entirely destroyed, we prefer to make peace at any terms!"

JIMMY CHRISTOPHER said thoughtfully: "I almost believe you are sincere."

Sinnott took a half step forward, exclaimed eagerly: "I tell you, we *are* sincere. We confined you here because we feared your influence on the rank and file of the people. Promise not to make any objections to the peace terms, and we will release you!"

Operator 5 did not hesitate. He rapped out: "No!"

Hartley put out an appealing hand. "Can't you understand, Operator 5? We don't want to see millions more slaughtered. Rudolph's guns can destroy every city in the country between the Mississippi and the Pacific. By making peace—"

Jimmy Christopher interrupted him quietly: "There is something you don't understand, Hartley. It is this—a country which has lost its honor might as well be extinct. You want to live—even as slaves. I don't want to live unless I can be free. That was the spirit in 1776. It's the spirit of most Americans today. All they need is a little spark of encouragement to go on fighting. That's what I've been trying to give them. America is a big country. It's true that Rudolph has guns and planes which we cannot match. It's true that he holds everything east of the Mississippi. But when he tries to conquer the rest of the country against a determined resistance, he'll find that his military organization isn't equal to it. Right now he's extended over a twenty-five hundred mile front." Jimmy's voice became pleading. "Let us fight every inch of ground. He'll have to spread out so thin that he won't be able to hold his organization together. Guerrilla warfare will beat him, even without guns. Don't you see that?"

Redfern shook his head. "We only see that millions of women

and children have already perished, and that if we don't make peace, millions more will die. No, Operator 5, our way is the only way. You must agree to fall in line with us."

"And if I don't?"

Redfern shrugged, glanced at his two companions. "There is only one alternative."

"My death?"

"Not exactly. Rudolph demands that we turn you over to him. He seems to have a particular hatred for you. We are going to do that."

Jimmy Christopher smiled. "You are a fool, Redfern. The men are loyal to the country, and they believe that I am the one to follow. It will surely become known that you have betrayed me. When that is discovered, the populace will rise against you and Rudolph, no matter what the odds. Then, of course, it will be too late for them to accomplish anything but get themselves killed. If you are sincere in what you say, Redfern, you can surely see that you will cause more destruction and death that way—"

Redfern stopped him. "We have thought of that, Operator 5. We have a solution."

While Jimmy Christopher watched him, tensely, the general bent and unwrapped the package he had placed upon the cot. "You see, we are going to steal a page from the book of a great novelist—Alexander Dumas!"

He held up for inspection the object he had removed from the package. It was round, hollow, and it opened on hinges at the back, with a clasp lock at the front. It was made exactly in the shape of a human head. There were two slits for the eyes, and a number of small air perforations at about the spot where the nose would fit. And there was a sort of hinged cap at the mouth—for feeding.

Jimmy Christopher said tightly: "You're going to put that on me?"

Redfern nodded. "No one shall see your face—even when you are Rudolph's prisoner! There will be no possible chance for anyone to learn that you are still alive. You will be the Man in the Iron Mask!"

He raised the devilish contrivance, stepped toward Operator 5.

Jimmy Christopher's eyes narrowed. He bent his knees, lunged at Redfern. But his feet were tied, his hands were tied, and his head was still whirling with his wound. Redfern stepped nimbly back, and Jimmy Christopher fell at his feet on the hard, cold floor. Blood began to flow once more from the wound at the back of his head. But he was still conscious.

With a last desperate effort he tried to struggle to his knees, but Sinnott and Hartley leaped upon him, pinned him down, while Redfern forced the iron mask over his head, snapped it shut and clicked the clasp lock. The face of Jimmy Christopher was hidden from the world.

Sinnott and Hartley sprang up as soon as the hideous device was securely fastened on the prostrate form of Operator 5. Sinnott was sweating. He rubbed the palms of his moist hands on his uniform, said hoarsely: "Let's get out of here!"

Redfern nodded. The three hurried out of the cell. Jimmy Christopher lay still. The shell of that iron mask had scraped the back of his head, opening the wound again. He felt himself growing weak. The cell door clanged to, leaving him in silence.

In the jail office, Admiral Sinnott and Colonel Hartley watched while Redfern picked up the phone, called for a number. In a moment he was talking to Count Leopold von Hauglein. He spoke in clipped accents, as if he had difficulty in controlling his voice.

"Count von Hauglein? The man you want is at your disposal. He is in solitary cell number four, here at the Barker Federal Penitentiary. What do you wish us to do with him?"

VON HAUGLEIN'S silky voice responded: "You have done very well, Redfern. I am sure my master will appreciate this. You have—er—followed my suggestion as to the mask?"

"Yes. The mask—is on."

"Good. Leave him there. Send me the key by either Admiral Sinnott or Colonel Hartley. You yourself should at once take charge of carrying out the balance of the terms of peace. You are now the active head of the defeated government; your president committed suicide a few minutes after you left."

Redfern gripped the receiver tightly. "What's that? The President—"

"Exactly. Perhaps it is better so. There will be less trouble with the populace. Now, if you will, please take charge of the troops which are evacuating the front line trenches. See that they are disarmed. And see that proper quarters and food are prepared for the Central Empire troops who will reach this city within an hour. Once we have taken over, I shall send your prisoner by plane to the emperor. That is all. Be sure to send me the key at once."

Slowly Redfern hung up. He turned to the other two. "Well, it's done. The President has killed himself. We three are in charge of all arrangements. I hope to God we can get the rest of the country to submit, so as to avoid further slaughter. You, Hartley, get the key of cell four from the warden, and take it to von Hauglein. Sinnott, stand guard in the corridor outside that cell, and don't let a soul approach until von Hauglein arrives. I'll do some phoning here, and then get out and take charge of turning over the city to Rudolph's troops."

Sinnott sighed deeply. "God, I'm glad that's over. I couldn't stand the look in Operator 5's eyes when he stood there in the cell and saw that mask. I—I feel like a traitor!"

Redfern laughed shortly. "It's the best thing for the country. Everything will go smoothly now. Rudolph should be merciful, since we have saved him the trouble of fighting. And that trouble-maker, Operator 5, is out of the way for good!"

He would not have spoken with such smug satisfaction if he had been privileged to see what was taking place outside the prison while he was making his call to von Hauglein.

The old Ford car which had followed him there was drawn up in the alley along the east wall of the prison. Whether by accident or design, it was parked in such a fashion that it completely blocked the view of the conduit box through which the telephone wires ran from the jail to the pole alongside it. In the shelter of the Ford, Slips McGuire knelt, with an earphone at his ear. The conduit box was open, and a line from the earphone was spliced into the telephone cable. He was listening closely.

Suddenly he took the instrument from his ear, and his long fingers swiftly undid the splicing. He closed the conduit box, picked up his paraphernalia, and came around to the front of the car, got in beside Diane Elliot who was sitting tensely at the wheel.

He was taut, excited. "Miss Elliot, they've got Jimmy in there. I didn't hear him say so in so many words, but if it wasn't Jimmy Christopher he was talking about, then I'm the King of Siam!" Hastily he recounted the conversation he had overheard between Redfern and von Hauglein. "And Hartley is gonna bring the key of this here cell to Hauglein. Now who else would they be so careful about?"

Diane gripped his arm. "Slips, we've got to find out whom they've got! We must get that key!"

Slips grunted. "Why don't we just get a bunch of guys together and tell 'em that Operator 5 is a prisoner in there? We could get up a nice raid on this here jail."

"No, Slips," Diane said. "It's too late for anything like that." She raised her hand, pointing up toward east. The sky had suddenly become black with dozens of huge transport planes. "There's the advance guard of the Central Empire, coming to occupy the city. Our boys are already falling back from the trenches, unarmed. If we started a raid it would only bring those

44

planes down on us. We've got to do it some other way. We've got to get the key. Now listen."

She lowered her voice, spoke swiftly. Slowly a grin grew on the thin face of Slips McGuire. "Let's go!" he exclaimed.

Diane threw the Ford into gear, drove around the corner, into the street in front of the jail. The staff car in which Redfern, Sinnott and Hartley had come was still standing close to the entrance. The street was crowded with ragged American soldiers, swarming toward the valley of the Kaw River. They had heard of the capitulation, and they were hurrying to get out of town before the Central Empire troops arrived. These youths, who had come from farms and timberland and coal mines to enlist in the defense of the nation, were disillusioned, broken in spirit by the news that Operator 5 was gone and that the General Staff had negotiated an abject surrender. There was no more fight in them.

DIANE SOUNDED her horn, drove through the crowd, and pulled up directly behind the staff car, so close that the bumpers of the two autos touched. Slips McGuire got out, swiftly crawled under the Ford, clutching a huge monkey wrench, and a small tire wrench. He did not remain under the Ford, but wormed his way forward until he was beneath the rear end of the staff car. He lay on his back, reached up with the monkey wrench and began to unscrew the bolts which held the inspection plate. His face grew red from the effort to loosen them, but once he got them started they came off easily, and the plate came down. Grease dripped on him, but he disregarded it. He pulled back the sleeve of his coat, reached up and inserted the tire wrench into the sprockets of the universal. Then he screwed the inspection plate on again.

He crawled back under the Ford, got out on the far side from the prison just as Colonel Hartley emerged from the doorway. The colonel got into the staff car, turned on the ignition, stepped on the starter, and shifted into gear. Slips McGuire climbed back into the rear of the Ford, leaned over Diane Elliot's shoulder and whispered: "Watch this!"

Diane's eyes were fastened on the staff car. She heard Hartley giving it gas, saw the car jerk forward. Then there was a tearing, rending sound of ripping gears, and the staff car ground to a stop less than three feet from where it had started.

Slips McGuire exclaimed: "It worked, Miss Elliot! It worked! Now do your stuff!"

Colonel Hartley was cursing under his breath, pushing up and down on the clutch, shifting experimentally from one speed to another. Each time he attempted to start there was a grinding of gears that sounded as if the inside of the car was being ripped out. He looked up helplessly as a cool young voice alongside him said: "Can I help you, Colonel?"

He looked up into the blue eyes of a pretty, chestnut-haired girl in the uniform of an ambulance driver. She was at the wheel of a Ford, and she was leaning out of the window, looking at him sympathetically.

Colonel Hartley grimaced. "I'm afraid something's happened to the insides of this car, Miss. And I'm in a hurry."

The girl said sweetly: "Can I give you a lift, Colonel?"

He kicked viciously at the clutch, swung out of the big car.

"Thanks. I've got to get over to the City Hall at once. It's important!"

"I'll be glad to drop you off. I was going that way to report to my unit." The girl pushed open the front door, and Hartley climbed in beside her. The girl smiled at him, started the Ford, and drove through the crowded street, turned left at the corner. Hartley was clutching a large key in his left hand, while with his right he was fingering the service revolver in his holster. He was eyeing the girl's shoulder straps.

"Look here, Miss," he suddenly exclaimed suspiciously, "you're with the third Field Unit of the Medical Corps. How is it you're not with your unit at Saint Louis? And why are you driving away from City Hall? Come to think of it, your face looks familiar. I know where I saw you—at Jacksonville. By Jove, you're Diane Elliot. You're Operator—"

He never got any further. From behind him a slender hand rose in the air, clutching a heavy monkey wrench. Another hand snatched off his cap, and the monkey wrench descended with a nasty crunch upon the back of his head. Colonel Hartley slumped in his seat without uttering a sound. And Slips McGuire said vindictively as he laid down the wrench: "That's one for Jimmy Christopher!"

Diane did not spare a glance at the inert form beside her. She drove steadily toward the less congested section of the city. She said over her shoulder: "As soon as we get to a quiet spot we'll dump the colonel, Slips. Be sure to get the key."

"I got it, Miss Elliot," Slips said. He had reached over and picked it off the seat where the good colonel had dropped it.

47

"You drive over to the Bottoms, Miss Elliot. We'll dump this guy in the mud. Then comes the hard part!"

Diane slowed down at an intersection, where masses of drifting, aimless American soldiers were milling about without direction or command, not knowing where to go or whom to turn to for orders. The crowds were as if stunned by the news of the surrender. Above them, enemy planes were droning in ever increasing numbers. And the wings of all those planes bore the dreadful insignia of the severed head and the crossed broadswords, the sign under which the Central Empire had conquered half of the world. That insignia meant more than just a banner. For Rudolph carried out in bloody deed the promise of the design upon his flag. And all these men were shuddering at the thought of the fate which must now reach out for those they loved.

Diane did not look up at the sky. She was busy honking at a motorcycle which had stopped in the middle of the intersection while the army officer who was driving it asked questions of the passing doughboys. Diane glanced nervously at the unconscious colonel beside her, said over her shoulder to Slips: "Of all times, they must pick this minute to stop there!"

SHE PRESSED her finger on the horn, kept it there. The horn sounded raucously, and the occupant of the side car attached to the motorcycle turned to glare at her. He was a huge man in the uniform of a sergeant. And Diane saw that he had a boy on his lap, who had been hidden from her by the sergeant's broad back. The sergeant frowned at her, bellowed something which she did not hear. She wasn't looking at the sergeant. She was gazing with almost unbelieving joy at the freckled face and pert Irish nose of the boy who sat in the sergeant's lap. Suddenly she emitted a shriek of joy.

"Tim! Timmy lad!" She kicked open the door of the car, pushed through the crowds of uniformed men toward that motorcycle. And Tim Donovan did a flying leap from Sergeant Geffen's lap out into the street. Diane threw her arms around the lad, and her eyes were wet. "Tim! I thought I'd never see you again! I thought you'd been captured or killed."

Tim Donovan's voice was a bit shaky, too. "Gee, Di, it's good to see you. You didn't have to worry about me. The Irish are hard to kill! Come on over and meet a couple of good friends of mine. And say—what about Jimmy? You got any idea where he might be?"

Behind them, Slips McGuire had pushed through the crowd. "Yeah, Tim, we got a good idea. And we got plans. But we could use some help. A couple husky guys!"

Tim grinned. "You can't find better than my two friends here—Lieutenant Bledsoe and Sergeant Geffen. Meet the original speed demons in person. We made it from the front line in an hour and five minutes!"

Bledsoe had climbed off the motorcycle and was standing with his hat in his hand, his eyes devouring the beautiful, slender figure of Diane Elliot. He took her hand when Tim introduced them, and held it a long time, looking into her eyes, until Diane lowered her own glance, and gently withdrew her hand. "Miss Elliot!" he exclaimed. And his eyes were shining with admiration, and with something else. "It was a lucky thing for me that I decided to escort Tim, here, from the front. Otherwise I'd never have met you!" Diane blushed a little under his ardent gaze. "If you and Sergeant Geffen will only lend us your help, Lieutenant."

"Anything, Miss Elliot. Anything at all. I'm entirely at your service!"

Slips McGuire broke in tartly. "You'll be glad to help us in this, Lieutenant. We're gonna try to get Miss Elliot's boyfriend out of a jam."

Bledsoe stiffened, turned to Slips. "Boyfriend?"

Diane broke in hastily: "He means Operator 5. We think he's being held prisoner in the Barker penitentiary. We're going to try to rescue him."

"I see," Bledsoe said dully. "Operator 5. I see."

"All right," Slips said crisply. "Let's get outta here. We got a guy with a staved in skull in the car that we gotta get rid of. And then we go to work. Let's get out of this crowd. Miss Elliot, you ride in that bathtub with the lieutenant, and Tim and the sergeant and I will take care of Hartley. Follow us up, and then we'll go into a huddle."

Bledsoe smiled, helped Diane into the side car. Diane felt the lieutenant's fingers on her arm, and she shivered slightly. She knew with a woman's instinct that she had without intention aroused something in Bledsoe that might prove troublesome at the least. Diane's whole soul was wrapped up in Jimmy Chris-

50

topher. She didn't like the lieutenant's caressing touch, the look in his eyes. Something cold within her warned her of disaster.

She managed a smile, seated herself in the side car and they drove off. Behind them, Tim Donovan drove the Ford, while Slips McGuire and Sergeant Geffen sat in the rear seat. The unconscious body of Colonel Hartley lay on the floor at Tim's feet.

And Sergeant Geffen said: "Say, Bledsoe sure fell like a ton of bricks for that young lady. You want to look out for him. He's a hell of a nice guy, but he's got a mean streak in him sometimes!"

CHAPTER 4
THE VENGEANCE OF RUDOLPH

THEY DIDN'T dump Colonel Hartley in the mud flats, as Slips McGuire had suggested. Instead, they took him to one of the shacks down near the packing house district, and left him there. These were homes of poor people, whose only pride in the world was their modest home; yet they were so fiercely in love with the idea of personal freedom that they had packed their belongings and made tracks for the west at the first hint of surrender on the part of the general staff. Rather than remain and bow to the conqueror, they had been willing to sacrifice those homes, and to move on westward. It was the spirit of these people which Jimmy Christopher had evaluated properly when he refused to agree to shameful peace; and it was this same spirit which Redfern and his associates, honest as they might be, had failed to comprehend.

51

Diane bandaged Hartley's head as best she could, and then the small group went into a council of war. Each of the five was taut with different emotions. Geffen, big, easy-going, square-faced, was perhaps the coolest of all. He knew his limitations. "My head," he said, grinning wryly, "wasn't made for schemes. You tell me what to do, Miss Elliot, and I'll do it. That's all I'm good for!"

Lieutenant Bledsoe wasn't much help, either, because it seemed that all he was capable of was to look constantly at Diane, to watch her every motion. Diane was embarrassed by his attention, wanted to tell him, before it went too far, that there was no chance in the world for him; that she belonged with every fiber of her soul to the man who was now in the Barker penitentiary. But she couldn't bring herself to do it. Perhaps if she had, much tragedy might have been averted later.

Now she was rapidly evolving a plan, with Tim and Slips making suggestions. Outside, enemy planes were coming over in ever increasing numbers. Past the shack there sped lorries with young American soldiers from the front, who were putting as much distance as possible between themselves and the advancing Central Empire troops. They had been told to disarm and evacuate the trenches. Well, many of them hadn't disarmed. They had defied their officers, who themselves were relaying the commands of the general staff in halfhearted fashion, and had commandeered lorries, motorcycles, cars, in order to leave the trenches with their arms. In their hearts there was still a faint hope that the word *finis* was not yet written to the fight for American freedom.

These boys were not singing and joking. Their faces, as Diane looked out of the window at them, were drawn with the weeks of privation and suffering, with the weeks of constant bombardment in the trenches. They were lean, hungry, but still tough. These boys, Diane thought, would be the nucleus for a last stand against the invader—if they could find someone worthy of leading them. And that somebody, she was sure, was at the present moment in a cell in the Federal penitentiary.

Slips McGuire and Tim were writing out a careful time schedule of the plan they had devised. Tim kept one, and gave the other to Bledsoe. Diane took a last look at the still unconscious Hartley, and then they all went outside. They shook hands. Geffen, Tim and Slips were going together in the Ford, Diane and Bledsoe in the motorcycle. Diane pressed Tim's hand, then that of Slips McGuire. "I hope it works, Slips. May God watch over you." Her eyes were wet as they parted, the Ford heading toward the penitentiary, the motorcycle toward the City Hall.

As the motorcycle climbed the slope of Kansas City toward the City Hall, there came to them the rolling of drums from the eastern section of the city—the drums of the advance guard of the first battalions of the conquering goose-stepping troopers of the Emperor Rudolph I, Emperor of the Central Empire, Lord of Europe and Asia, and conqueror of America.

Diane shuddered in the side car. She said, in a small voice which Bledsoe had difficulty in hearing: "There are only the five of us—standing between the misery of our country and the mightiest emperor the world has ever seen!"

Bledsoe raced the motorcycle. His face reflected a queer fight of devotion as he looked sideways at her. "It's a ticklish job, Miss Elliot. But I'd do more than this for you. I'd do anything in the world for you. If we fail, or if I am killed, I want you to know that—"

Diane stopped him, speaking hastily: "We must not be killed—yet. And we can't fail. God is on our side!"

JIMMY CHRISTOPHER lay very still for a long time after Redfern, Sinnott and Hartley left his cell. How long he lay there, he didn't know. It might have been a minute, an hour or a day. He was not entirely unconscious. That wound in his head, aggravated as it was by the friction of the iron mask, was enough to have finished an ordinary man. But Operator 5 was tough. The very kind of life he led was one which inured him to hardship, to pain. He had schooled himself ever to force his mind to continue to function against all odds, just as he had hardened his body to go on in the face of agony, danger and apparently insurmountable obstacles. Often in the past it had been that last unsuspected degree of vitality, of hidden reserve, which had won for him a battle over an astounded adversary who had been sure he was through.

Now, Jimmy Christopher's mind swam hazily, while he fought back to consciousness. The stone floor was cold against his naked torso. His wrists burned where the thongs cut cruelly

Tim Donovan

into them, behind his back. He knew why he had been stripped of his upper clothes. It was known to Redfern that he usually carried implements of queer kinds which had often aided him to escape from precarious, sometimes hopeless situations. And Redfern was taking no chance.

Jimmy Christopher smiled grimly in the dark behind his hideous mask. He moved his wrists experimentally, and an acute twinge of pain shot through his arms. He turned over on his right side, and a great, overwhelming roaring sound beat against the inside of his head as if it would burst out of his cranium. He gasped, lay still for a while, until the roaring subsided, leaving only a deep, throbbing pain that seemed to be everywhere at once, from the nape of his neck around in a sheet of dull agony to his eyes.

But he began to move his body again, purposefully. He slowly drew up his knees, arching his back as he did so, until they were touching the chin of his metal mask. Then, still lying on his right side, he drew back his heels, pushing down with his bound wrists. He was trying to get his wrists down under his feet and around in front of him. At last, heels and wrists met. He hooked his wrists around the heels of his shoes, left them there, lying still doubled up, panting for breath, closing his eyes to lull the pain in his head.

After a few moments he started again. Inch by inch he moved his wrists down along the soles of his shoes toward the tips. At last he was rewarded with success. His hands were in front of him, though it was true that they were still bound together.

His fingers and hands were numb. He flexed his fingers and raised them to the mask, groped toward the lock. He felt a little tumbler alongside the nose perforations, and his lips behind the mask set grimly. The two halves of the mask were locked by an ingenious little combination lock. He had wondered about that, for he had heard no key turned when Redfern locked it. By moving his head a little inside the mask, he could feel the small lock. There was no way to open it without the combination, unless it were hammered off him.

He shrugged, and his hands descended to the belt of his trousers. He smiled tightly. Redfern *had* overlooked one bet. Jimmy Christopher's fingers fumbled with the buckle of the belt. He released it, and the whole belt seemed to spring away like a coiled snake striking, and then it straightened out. Jimmy swished it through the air, and the leather slid off, revealing in his hand a bright, keen blade of Toledo steel which had rested inside that leather sheath-belt. It was this rapier that had more than once saved Jimmy Christopher's life. His eyes were gleaming through the slits of the mask as he knelt painfully, held the blade upright between his knees, and began to cut away at the bonds on his wrists.

In a moment the keen steel had cut through them. Jimmy forgot about his throbbing head as he reversed the blade, slashed efficiently at the bonds on his ankles. And then he stood erect, breathing deeply, unfettered except for the horrid mask over his head. The mask was not heavy. It was made of some clever alloy that was strong, yet light of weight.

Carefully Jimmy Christopher recovered the leather sheath, slid the rapier into it and attached it once more about his waist. Somewhere outside, where the sun was shining, he could hear the droning of airplanes, the beating of drums. He knew that they were not American planes, for the United States had no such quantities left. He knew also that the drums were those of the Central Empire. They could mean only one thing—that the Central Empire was marching into Kansas City. His hands clenched at his sides. He began to move about the cell, feeling the walls.

And just then he heard confused sounds in the corridor, followed by hurrying footsteps. The steps stopped at the grilled door. Jimmy couldn't see out there, but he grimly drew his rapier once more, moved over to a position where he could run through the first person that stepped inside the door. With the rolling of those drums, and the buzz of those airplanes, there was no mercy in the soul of Operator 5 for his jailers. He was going to kill as many of them as he could before he died.

A KEY was fitted into the lock, and slowly the door began to swing open. A form appeared, and Jimmy Christopher lunged, sending the point of his rapier unerringly toward the throat of the man who stood there. But suddenly a dim shaft of light from somewhere fell athwart the countenance of the man whose life was about to be snuffed out. Jimmy saw his face, uttered a quick cry, and swished his rapier to one side with a powerful flick of the wrist. The blade slid past the man's neck, and Jimmy shouted hoarsely:

"Slips McGuire! You son-of-a-gun! Why don't you announce yourself?"

Slips McGuire, blinking into the frightful figure of the half-naked man with the hideous mask on his face and the flickering sword in his hand, exclaimed: "Jimmy Christopher! God! What've they done to you?" Jimmy Christopher suddenly burst out laughing, happily. "Slips, you never looked like an angel to me before. But right at this minute, all you need is a pair of wings!"

"B-but Jimmy! What's that thing on you? What were they doing to you?"

58

"Nothing much, Slips. They were just trying to bury me—in an iron mask!"

Behind Slips there appeared the big, burly form of Sergeant Geffen. He was carrying on his shoulder the unconscious form of Admiral Sinnott. Jimmy Christopher moved back into the cell, and Slips and Geffen came in.

"Don't make too much noise, Jimmy," Slips warned. "If we're caught, we're—*plunk!*" He clucked his palate on the word to indicate what he meant.

"How'd you get in here?" Jimmy demanded.

Slips grinned, keeping his eyes on the mask. "Say, Jimmy, you look like a lost soul in that thing. How'd we get in here? Easy. I snipped the telephone wires outside, and then Sergeant Geffen and I came in and said we were telephone men. They let us in, and we worked over to this section. Sinnott here was standing guard in the corridor, but Geffen smacked him, and presto, here we are! Tim is outside with our car—if we can get out of here again. It was easier coming in."

Geffen put the unconscious body of Sinnott on the cot. "Search him," said Jimmy, "and see if you can find the combination to this damned thing on my head." While Geffen was looking through Sinnott's pockets, Jimmy asked: "What's the situation outside, Slips? Is it—the end?"

Slips nodded somberly. "I'm afraid so, Jimmy. Rudolph's troops are marching into the city. Redfern has ordered the boys to disarm and leave the trenches. But there's a lot of people that still want to fight."

"Well," Jimmy Christopher said grimly, "we'll see if we can't do something about that! Now, about getting out."

Slips broke in. "Miss Elliot worked out a plan for that. Now look, Jimmy—"

He stopped abruptly as footsteps sounded in the corridor....

COUNT LEOPOLD VON HAUGLEIN sat in the room in the City Hall where the President of the United States had taken his own life less than an hour ago. The pitiful body had been removed, and the worthy count was beaming upon a small group of Central Empire officers who had arrived with the first contingent of planes. "Gentlemen," he addressed them, "the rest of the United States is ours. We have only to march to the Pacific. The Americans will offer us no resistance. Their president is dead, our foremost opponent is a prisoner in our hands, and the commanding officers of their armies have agreed to our terms. They hope that the emperor will be merciful!"

The officers laughed. One of them exclaimed: "I always knew that Americans were fools! To expect mercy from the emperor is to expect that the lion will cease to roar, or that the tides will fail to rise. The emperor hates these Americans bitterly."

Von Hauglein smiled in smug satisfaction. "That fool of a Redfern has delivered our worst enemy, Operator 5, into my hands. Operator 5 is even now a prisoner. Redfern is sending me the key to his cell in the Barker penitentiary where the man is being held. The emperor will be particularly pleased with that. And another thing, gentlemen!" His eyes twinkled wickedly. "The American women here in the West, they tell me, are even more beautiful than those in the East. They are delicious morsels. We should have a *very* pleasant time here!"

The others joined in his laughter, flattering him, praising him for his clever diplomacy and his eye for women.

Already these sycophants were fawning upon one whom they saw likely to become an imperial favorite.

Von Hauglein became crisp. He examined telegraphic reports on his desk.

"Let us see, now. Marshal Kremer is moving forward along the entire front.

This city is now in our hands. We will make it our headquarters until the marshal arrives. We must take over all food stores at once, and—"

He was interrupted by the entrance of a sub-officer who reported that a young woman in the uniform of an American ambulance driver sought to speak to him.

Van Hauglein frowned. "A woman? What does she want?"

"She says that she has a message and a key from a Colonel Hartley, Excellency."

"Ah, yes. Bring her in."

Von Hauglein rubbed his hands. "It is the key to the cell where Operator 5 is being held!"

OUTSIDE, DIANE ELLIOT was glancing at her watch as the officer came to show her into van Hauglein's presence. Lieutenant Bledsoe, who stood beside her, glanced at the time schedule which Tim Donovan had worked out, and said: "We're right on the dot, Miss Elliot, to the minute. If McGuire, and

Geffen and the boy have done their end of it, it ought to go off like clockwork."

The sub-officer came out from von Hauglein's office, motioned to Diane to follow him. Bledsoe waited outside. In the office, the Central Empire officers cast admiring glances at Diane's trim figure. She advanced to the desk, forcing a smile, and extended the key that had been taken from Hartley.

"Colonel Hartley asked me to bring this to you, sir," she told him quietly. "The colonel said you would know what it was."

Von Hauglein took the key. "Yes, yes, of course. But where is Colonel Hartley? He was to come personally."

Diane had been expecting the question. "The colonel has had a slight accident with his car, sir. He was—injured. I was passing, and he asked me to perform the mission for him."

Von Hauglein had arisen from his seat behind the desk, and his eyes were wandering over Diane's figure. "Thank you, Miss." He turned to the other officers. "Gentlemen, excuse me. I must go to visit the person I mentioned to you before. You will await my return?"

They bowed. Diane started for the door, but von Hauglein stopped her. "Not so fast, young lady. I like your looks. Won't you stay here till I return?"

Diane flushed under his gaze. "I'd rather not!"

Suddenly his smile vanished. He took a quick step forward, seized her wrist. It's not a question of what you would rather do!" he said harshly. "You are an American. We are the visitors. You will do as I command. Kindly remain!"

Diane glanced desperately from him to the amused officers

who were watching. They threw facetious comments at von Hauglein. "You have excellent taste, Count. I wish I had seen her first! A pretty thing, isn't she? We'll hold her for you, von Hauglein! Will you trust her in our care?"

The count scowled at them. "Why don't you go out and get your own? The whole city is at your feet. There are plenty of women. And His Imperial Majesty permits us to go as far as we like. But keep away from this one. I have taken a fancy to her!"

Diane shrank away from him, turned to dash for the door. Von Hauglein ripped out a curse, went after her. Diane was almost through the doorway when the sub-officer who had shown her in stepped in front of her. Diane brought up short, and von Hauglein caught her by the shoulder, sent her spinning into the room. "Keep her here!" he commanded the sub-officer. "And I will take no excuses from you if she's gone when I return!"

He stormed out of the room, and hurried downstairs. Bledsoe, near the front entrance, saw him pass, and looked back anxiously when he saw that Diane was not with him. Their plan had contemplated Diane's coming out with von Hauglein and going to the penitentiary with him. Bledsoe was worried about Diane. Instead of following von Hauglein, he started upstairs in search of Diane. He was not stopped. There were dozens of American officers in the building, assisting the Central Empire commanders to take over the city, and arranging for turning over supplies. These men were moving about with set, hopeless faces. They were carrying out orders, like good soldiers. But they could see already, from the attitudes of the Imperial officers, that the vanquished would receive little consideration.

It was the presence of these American officers that made it easy for Bledsoe to wander about the building looking for Diane. And it was that search of his which was to have such tragic consequences a few days later.

In the meantime, von Hauglein commandeered a car and a squad of Central Empire troops, and drove across the city toward the penitentiary.

The United States flag over the jail had been hauled down, and in its place there waved the black banner of the Central Empire with its gruesome insignia of the severed head and crossed broadswords. Everywhere now, gray-clad goose-stepping troops were moving through the streets, and Americans slunk along, hugging the buildings. Now and then a shot would ring out. An American who had failed in show of respect to the conqueror would double over and thresh out his life on the pavement. Von Hauglein smiled. This was the way to treat these dogs, he thought.

INSIDE THE penitentiary, he met General Redfern in the warden's office. The general's face was drawn, pale. "I have kept my bargain, Count," he said to von Hauglein. "The city is yours, and Operator 5 is a prisoner. You will remember your promise to show mercy to our people?"

Von Hauglein smiled thinly. "The emperor will know how to thank you, Redfern. I am leaving the subordinate positions in charge of Americans whom you approve of. See to it that all whom you retain are willing to pledge loyalty to the emperor. You are making this your headquarters?"

"For the time being," Redfern told him. "I shall do my best to convince the populace that they should acknowledge Rudolph." His eyes were rimmed with red, mirroring a deep inward struggle. "I hope to God that I'm doing the right thing!"

Von Hauglein clapped him on the back. "Of course you are, Redfern. The emperor may find it necessary to be a little severe at the beginning, but after we have consolidated the new government, the people of the country will thank you for having saved them from utter destruction. And now," he rubbed his hands, "where is this Operator 5?"

"I'll take you to him."

"No, no. I have two troopers with me. I wish to see him alone, for just a moment—" his lips twisted into a cruel smile—"to tell him confidentially what kind of reception the emperor is preparing for him. Then we shall take him away. Tomorrow the emperor arrives. And between you and me, Redfern, you have done a good piece of work for yourself in arranging this gift of the person of Operator 5 for His Imperial Majesty. I happen to know that the Emperor would rather watch Operator 5's execution than add another kingdom to his empire!"

Redfern shuddered at the gloating look in von Hauglein's eye. "I'm truly sorry for Operator 5. But I suppose his execution will be a small price to pay for sparing a whole nation. And if I should find any favor in the emperor's eyes, I shall use it to influence him to be as lenient as possible with a conquered country."

"Yes, yes, of course," von Hauglein said absently. "Now, this Operator 5—where will I find him?"

"In the east wing, Count. I have had him placed in the solitary section. No jailers are permitted near him. The only man in that wing now is Admiral Sinnott, who has the combination of that mask, if you should want it."

Von Hauglein bowed hastily, and left the office, motioning to the two troopers who were waiting for him in the corridor.

Redfern watched him through the open door of the office, until Hauglein and the troopers had disappeared around a bend. He sat there, gray-faced, for fifteen minutes. The telephone rang continuously during that time, and he answered it mechanically, instructing the American division commanders who reported to withdraw their troops from the trenches and to leave all arms and ammunition for the disposal of the advancing Central Empire troops. His voice was low, broken. To those commanders who protested at the order, he made the same stereotyped reply:

"Do you think I like this any more than you do? My God, man, it's harder for me to order you to do this than for you to obey. It's I who have to carry all the responsibility for the surrender. Believe me, we couldn't hold out another day. And we'll get more consideration from Emperor Rudolph this way than if we anger him by further useless opposition. Believe me, we have no alternative!"

But there was one phone call which Redfern couldn't handle that way. It was long distance from Los Angeles, and the voice of the man at the other end rapped into his ear in sharp, staccato, accusing phrases: "Redfern! What's this I hear about surrender? Is it true?"

Redfern frowned. "Who the devil is this?"

PATRIOTS' DEATH BATTALION

"This is Z-7—calling from Los Angeles!* I just got word over an amateur radio network** that you have ordered the evacua-

---

* AUTHOR'S NOTE: A little later on in this chronicle we shall meet at closer range the strange man who is known by no name except the symbol, Z-7. Most readers of the exploits recorded in this magazine are familiar with the part played by Z-7 in the history of American espionage. Those readers who have picked this magazine up for the first time will find an informative footnote concerning this remarkable man, appended to the text in Chapter Six. I am placing the footnote there rather than here, since Z-7 does not properly enter the story till then.

** AUTHOR'S NOTE: At the end of the third week of the invasion, the radio communication systems of the nation were seriously crippled. Most of the Eastern Seaboard was in the hands of the Central Empire, and the large radio stations had either been taken over by the emperor or destroyed. Telephone, telegraph and radio communication from the east to the presidential headquarters and to the west coast was reduced to zero. No news was filtering through as to the state of affairs in the occupied territory, and men and women throughout the nation were frantically trying to secure information about their loved ones in the devastated zones. It was then that amateur radio really came into its own. Prior to that time it has served usefully in times of flood and earthquake (in this connection there is an interesting article in the May, 1936, issue of *Reader's Digest)*. But now amateur radio truly became an integral part of national defense. Almost overnight a nationwide network of amateur radio stations were hooked up, largely through the efforts of Nan Christopher, Operator 5's twin sister, of whom we shall hear more anon. Accounts of the atrocities in the occupied territory buzzed from the ether. Young men in shacks and farm houses watched the passage of Rudolph's

67

tion of the trenches in the absence of Operator 5. Damn you, Redfern, by what authority did you do that? Where's the President? Surely he never consented—"

"The President has approved of the peace terms, Z-7!" Redfern said stiffly. "I don't know what business it is of yours."

"I'm making it my business! Redfern, you've betrayed the country. You always hated Operator 5. I shouldn't be surprised if you had a hand in his disappearance!"

THE GENERAL gripped the receiver tight, his face flushed a deep red. "You're mad, Z-7! The situation was hopeless. There was nothing else to be done!"

"Hopeless, eh?" The voice coming across the wire from the coast was filled with scorn. It wouldn't have been hopeless if Operator 5 had remained on the scene. *Redfern, what have you done with Operator 5?*"

Redfern licked his dry lips with his tongue. That Z-7 should have guessed any part of the secret he shared with Sinnott and Hartley was startling. Though Z-7 was a thousand miles away, Redfern shuddered at the ominous way in which the question was asked.

And just then the sweating general saw four figures round

troops, and sent accurate reports of their numbers and equipment through a series of interlocked air stations, using a code which Operator 5 devised. Many of these young men were apprehended and executed by Rudolph's agents; but there were always more to carry on. And it was through this channel that the West first learned of the shameful peace terms negotiated by the General Staff.

the bend in the corridor, coming from the direction of the solitary wing. In the lead strutted the pompously uniformed figure of Count Leopold von Hauglein. Behind him came the two troopers, supporting between them a half-unconscious figure whose head was encased in a metal mask.

Redfern closed his eyes to shut out the sight. They must have handled Operator 5 pretty roughly to have to support him this way. When he opened his eyes, the four figures had passed the open door of his office, on the way to the side exit. They were probably going to spirit their prisoner out with as much secrecy as possible. Z-7's crackling voice was still scorching the wire: "You know what I think, Redfern? I think you've either killed Operator 5, or are holding him prisoner somewhere, so you'll have a free hand in betraying your country. I'm going to fly east and look into this myself; and by God, Redfern, if I find I'm right, I'll break your neck with my own two hands!"

Redfern almost shrieked into the phone: "I swear to you, Z-7, that I am not holding Operator 5 a prisoner. And I haven't killed him. I tell you, I haven't. I—"

He stopped. The line was dead.

All through that day and the next, Redfern couldn't rid himself of the vision in his memory of the four figures moving down the corridor. He had never seen Operator 5 except with his head in the air, proudly alive with a moving vitality. Redfern hated Operator 5, as Z-7 had said. But he could get no consolation out of the thought of Operator 5 being almost carried along the corridor by those two troopers. He, Redfern, was the cause of that. He had betrayed the man he hated. But it was not

because he hated him; it was to save his country from misery—
or so he told himself.

The next day, Rudolph entered Kansas City at the head of his
victorious cohorts, and rape and pillage began. Redfern paled to
hear the atrocities that were being committed, but he was helpless to stop them. He went in search of von Hauglein to protest,
but found that the count was not in the city, and he could get no
information as to his whereabouts.

Redfern was in complete charge of the liaison work between
the conquered and the conquerors. All orders as to disposition
of supplies were transmitted to him from Marshal Kremer. He
found himself in a position where he had to promulgate decrees
which nauseated him. In the privacy of his office he wept at the
things that were being done to his countrymen. Too late he
realized his mistake. But he was a man in a trap—a trap of his
own making. He could not withdraw from his new duties, lest
he antagonize Rudolph and bring down harsher measures upon
his people. He wept in the privacy of his office, wishing that Z-7
would make good his threat and come and kill him.

And in the meantime the Emperor of the Central Empire
proceeded to grind his heel into the bleeding body of a
conquered nation.

For two days after Rudolph moved into Kansas City, there
was written across the country a bloody chapter which history
will ever blush to record. And on the very day when Rudolph
and his retinue occupied the huge Convention Hall where Pres-
idents of the United States had once been nominated, there was
enacted a drama which will always be narrated in text books

wherever American history is taught, and which will become part of our glorious legends.

THAT MORNING, the sun rose as brightly as it had on every other morning. The fact that the knell of American independence had been rung seemed not to have affected the solar system whatsoever. In the street in front of Convention Hall, there was a buzz of activity. Tall scaffolding was being erected, buttressed by struts fixed to the Convention building. Two tall derricks had been moved close to the scaffolding, and the street was roped off at either end, guarded by gray-clad troopers of the Central Empire.

Crowds of moodily silent Americans watched the proceedings, fearful to ask what was going on lest they invite a bayonet in the throat. Presently, a great truck pulled into the street, and a great gasp went up from the populace as they saw what the truck was bringing.

It was a huge bell.

A murmur ran through the crowd—a murmur of resentment, which was quickly stilled when a Central Empire officer gave the order to fix bayonets. That murmur of resentment was occasioned by the fact that the crowd had recognized the bell. The long crack in it identified it as the Liberty Bell, removed by Rudolph from Independence Hall in Philadelphia and transported behind his advancing regiments, to be set up in each city that was occupied. It served as a grim reminder to the American people that the symbol of their liberty was now in alien hands.

Workmen—Americans commandeered from among the captives—were driven to aid in the work of raising the huge bell, which weighed more than a ton, so that it could be suspended from the top of the scaffolding. While this was going on, the Emperor Rudolph was sitting in state upon the dais inside Convention Hall. The rows upon rows of seats had been removed, and in the cleared space there now stood several hundred captives. They were a bedraggled, forlorn group, huddled together under the guns of ever watchful guards. They looked sullenly, hopelessly toward the dais where the emperor sat. At Rudolph's right was the stiff, ramrod figure of Marshal Kremer, the man whose military genius had brought the Imperial armies across half the United States. The marshal's face was set, stern. His military tunic was decorated with a dozen medals.

At Rudolph's left stood a beautiful, dark-haired woman. She also wore a military tunic, and riding breeches. The tunic was tight, setting off to advantage the rounded contours of her body. Her chin was firm, stubborn; her nose straight, and her mouth small. Her dark hair was pinned at the back of her head in a huge coil. She was the girl who had flown Tim Donovan over the lines the day before. She was Rudolph's cousin, but she did not resemble him in any way.

A little to one side there was a small group of courtiers, all in uniform, and all watching the emperor.

Rudolph let his gaze rove over the captives. He ran his tongue around the edges of his lips, and there was a cruel glint in his eyes. He beckoned to one of his officers, said: "Have Operator 5 and the others brought in at once!"

The officer bowed, and left. Rudolph glanced around him, frowned. "Where is Von Hauglein?" he demanded. "I want him here! It was he who brought about the capture of Operator 5. I am going to reward him!"

Marshal Kremer grimaced distastefully. "He is nowhere about, Your Majesty. No doubt he has found some fair companion among the captives."

Rudolph smirked. "Von Hauglein always was a lady's man, Kremer. You envy him. I think you'd be more pleasant if you would unbend once in a while. Why don't you pick yourself some presentable female?" He winked toward his cousin, but she did not seem to have heard him. "There are really plenty to choose from."

Kremer's face remained set sternly. "Someone has to pay attention to business, sire. If I did as Hauglein does, who would win your battles for you?"

Rudolph's face flushed. "You begin to think you are indispensable, don't you, Kremer?"

"Fortunately, I am, sire. Otherwise, I am afraid my head should have been in a basket long ago."

"You are impertinent!"

"I am sorry, sire. I am not a courtier. I am a soldier!"

Rudolph's hands were clenched. His lips were quivering with rage, "You—"

A cool hand on his arm stopped him. The dark young woman said soothingly: "Please, Rudolph, leave Kremer alone. He is loyal to you, even if he doesn't know how to control his tongue."

Rudolph glared at her. "You are all in a conspiracy against me!" he whined. "Wasn't it you who helped that boy to escape? I ought to have you beheaded for that!" His unstable mind had already forgotten Marshal Kremer. "Be careful, Anita. Don't try me too far. One day I may order you to the chopping block, cousin or no cousin!"

MARSHAL KREMER nodded his thanks to the girl. She smiled, turned her big dark eyes full on the emperor.

"You can have me beheaded, Rudolph, but you won't. You like me too well for that!"

The emperor's glare turned into a grudging smile. "You're a witch, Anita. And damn you, you are beautiful. When will you marry me?"

"Not till you've stopped this meaningless bloodshed and torture!" For a moment her eyes glinted with loathing, then she quickly veiled them, forced a smile.

Rudolph seemed to be torn between admiration for her and the sadistic instinct within himself. "Soon, Anita, soon. When I am absolute master of the earth, I shall stop all this. Then you'll marry me? I'll make you empress of the world. I know you don't love me; but to be empress of the world, a woman will do much, eh?"

Anita looked speculatively out over the heads of the huddled captives in the center of the great hall. "Sometimes, Rudolph, I think I will never marry you. I should hate to wake up in the middle of the night and find that you were driving red hot needles under my toenails!"

"Ha, ha!" Rudolph laughed loud, uproariously, and the courtiers behind him, though they had not heard the conversation, laughed also, in chorus. Only Marshal Kremer did not laugh. The old soldier's gaunt face was glum, sour. His eyes met Anita's once more. They both knew that she had deliberately diverted the emperor's attention from the marshal. All the imperial court knew that she was the only person who was able, even to a small degree, to curb the emperor's moments of mad fury when he was capable of consigning his closest courtiers to hours of torture followed by merciful death. Even she, however, had not been able to cause Rudolph to ease up on the American captives.

Kremer himself, with his blunt tongue, had more than once placed himself in the shadow of imperial displeasure; and had been saved from swift, painful punishment by the fact that the crusty old marshal was the only one whom Rudolph could safely rely upon to push the conquest of America to a satisfactory conclusion. And on the occasions when Rudolph's blind fury at some remark of Kremer's caused the emperor to forget how much he needed the marshal, Anita Monfred had turned the emperor's displeasure away from thoughts of vengeance. The marshal had been loyal to Maximilian, and would remain loyal to Rudolph. The girl shrank from the idea of marrying the madman who occupied the throne of the Central Empire, but she had no alternative. As well might she have tried to escape from her shadow as to escape to any part of the world where Rudolph's arm could not reach today.

So between these two there was a sort of tacit alliance.

Now the attention of all three, as well as that of the courtiers, was turned toward the small group of three people that was being escorted across the floor. Heavily guarded by gray-clad troopers, two of those three marched with their heads up, staring defiantly toward the imperial dais. The third figure strug-

75

gled violently in the hands of two soldiers. The captives in the center of the hall watched the three with wide, compassionate eyes.

The officer in charge of the guards stepped up to the dais, bowed low. "Your imperial majesty, here are the three special prisoners. The one in the metal mask who is struggling so violently with his guards—" the officer lowered his voice—"is Operator 5. None of the Americans suspects who he is. According to Count von Hauglein's orders, that mask was placed upon his head. The count was fearful lest the populace

And now the man in the iron
mask was hanging by the neck,
his feet jerking in the air....

should get out of hand if they learned that their national idol was to be executed."

Rudolph shrugged, glancing toward the masked, struggling figure. "What do we care what the populace does? Let them rise. We can mow them down with machine guns. But—" he grinned wickedly—"keep that mask on. I like the idea. Can he talk through it?"

The officer shook his head. "No, sire. He is gagged under the mask."

Rudolph glanced to either side, at Anita and at Marshal Kroner. His eyes were glowing wickedly. "This is the moment that I have been waiting for! I shall make von Hauglein the Viceroy of America as a reward for sending him here. It will be a pleasure to watch him die—in the special way that I thought out all by myself!"

Anita said scornfully: "I'm sure it's a very original way, Rudolph. You are very good at those things. Who are the other two people with Operator 5? That girl is very beautiful."

The officer explained. "The girl is Diane Elliot. She was being held at Count von Hauglein's orders, when one of our men recognized her. She is the one person whom Operator 5 would give his life to save."

RUDOLPH INTERRUPTED him, laughing gleefully. "So! We have him, and we have his woman! Who is that young fool in lieutenant's uniform, with her?"

"That, sire, is a certain Lieutenant Bledsoe. While the Elliot girl was being held, he fought his way into our midst in the City

Hall Building, and attempted to rescue her—singlehanded. We captured him, as you see, sire."

"H'm." He motioned the officer away. "Take the three of them outside. Take all these captives out. They shall witness the special execution I have arranged for Operator 5, and then they will themselves be beheaded—"

Anita stopped him. "But, Rudolph! Why must you behead all these men?"

"These men, my dear, are the mayors of the various towns which resisted us. There are two hundred of them. When they are beheaded, we will see if the mayors of other towns are so eager to fight for their country!"

The prisoners were being herded out. Anita impulsively left Rudolph's side, and hastened over to Diane Elliot. Her guards stood at respectful attention while the two girls faced each other. There was no flicker of fear in Diane's clear eyes as she met those of Anita Monfred. "You must be the girl who flew Tim Donovan across the lines," Diane guessed.

Anita nodded.

"That was a brave thing," Diane said. "I want to thank you for it."

Anita laughed. "You don't have to thank me. I did it for a whim. I wanted to see how far I could goad my cousin."

"Then what do you want with me?"

"I just wanted to take a good look at you." Anita's English was almost as good as Diane's, except for the slightest hint of a slur. "I've heard so much about this Operator 5 of yours—" she threw a glance at the struggling figure in the hideous mask, who was

79

being forced outside along with the captive mayors and Lieutenant Bledsoe—"that I wanted to see what kind of woman a man like Operator 5 could be so much in love with!"

"Well, now you know," Diane said flatly.

"Now I know," Anita breathed. "And now I would like to see the face of Operator 5. I have never seen him. He must be quite a man. I wonder if Rudolph would consent to take his mask off before he is executed."

Diane flared up. "Can't you let him die, even, without torturing him? Isn't Rudolph doing enough to him, without your adding to his humiliation?"

Anita laughed. She waved to the guards to take Diane out. "Perhaps," she called out, "if I see him and like his looks, I'll try to save him—for myself!"

Outside, the workmen had finished their work. The huge bell was in its place on the scaffolding, hanging with its mouth but a few feet from the ground. Alongside the scaffolding, was a second, smaller scaffold, upon which rested four chopping blocks in a row. These were for the wholesale executions that Rudolph had promised. Central Empire soldiers with bayonets fixed lined both sides of the street, keeping the surly crowd in check.

The pitiful crowd of captive mayors was herded up close to the chopping blocks where they knew their heads were soon to rest. Diane and her two fellow captives were close at the side of the big Liberty Bell. Diane was looking at it with dawning horror. Her eyes met those of Bledsoe, and the lieutenant gave her a hopeless glance. She said, very low: "Thanks, lieutenant, for your gallant attempt to rescue me. It is going to cost you your life."

"It doesn't matter, Miss Elliot. It's you—if I could only save you!"

Diane's eyes filmed, she turned to the Man in the Iron Mask. "Jimmy!" she murmured. "What a way for you to die—you, who always hoped to die with a gun in your hand!"

SHE SHUDDERED. They had thrown an old army coat over the bare torso of their Man in the Iron Mask, and the soldiers were making facetious remarks in their own guttural language.

Suddenly, the voice of Emperor Rudolph sounded loud from the steps of the Convention Hall, where he stood, surrounded by his officers, talking into a microphone connected with amplifiers along the street.

"Men of America!" he said. "You see before you your own precious Liberty Bell—" his lips twisted in scorn—"which has always been the symbol of your liberty. Today it shall sound the signal of your submission to us—Rudolph I, Emperor of Europe, Asia and America. That man—" he pointed across the street—"in the Iron Mask is going to die today. You do not know who he is. You shall be informed—after his death. And then you will realize that your last hope is gone. Then let the word go out to your brothers and fathers and friends and relatives in the Far West that it is better to submit than to resist. Now—" he waved a hand—"proceed with the execution!"

Two men stepped out from alongside the Liberty Bell. With rough hands they pushed Diane and Bledsoe aside, seized the

Man in the Iron Mask and dragged him over underneath the bell. The knocker had been removed, and a stout length of hemp hung in its place, with a loop at the end. Other soldiers stepped up, and soon the noose was slipped over the captive's neck. His feet barely touched the ground. His hands were tied behind his back. The soldiers stepped back, looked toward Rudolph.

The emperor was arguing heatedly with Anita Monfred, while Marshal Kremer and the courtiers watched. Anita's eyes were blazing. "I tell you, Rudolph, I want to see the face of Operator 5 before you hang him!"

Rudolph, sulky, sullen, shook his head stubbornly. "And I tell you, Anita, you shall not see him. That man is going to die just like that!"

"Rudolph, I shall never talk to you again!"

"Ha! You'll talk to me, all right."

She turned away from him, her eyes blazing, and shouted to the soldiers under the bell:

"Take off that—"

A backhanded blow from Rudolph sent her staggering into the arms of Marshal Kremer. And Rudolph raised a hand, ordered:

"Proceed!"

Anita was panting with anger, quivering. Kremer pressed her shoulder with a gnarled hand. "Why do you insist on this, Baroness? What will you gain by seeing the face of Operator 5? I have seen him. He is a handsome young man, nothing more. You—"

Anita was breathing hard. "I—I don't know myself, why I

82

want to see his face. It—it's the things I've heard about him. They're so marvelous. I could admire a man who has done the things that he has done."

Kremer laughed. "In love with a name, eh? Well, it's too late!"

They had raised the rope in the bell, and now the captive was hanging by the neck, his feet off the ground, the knot of the noose just behind his left ear.

Rudolph was laughing gleefully. "Look! See him twitch. He'll take a long time dying!"

Slowly, the great bell began to move from side to side. Its mouth described a longer and longer arc, until the feet of the twitching man were striking against the sides. Metal spurs had been attached to the victim's shoes, so that each time his heels struck, the bell emitted a *bong*.

Rudolph was dancing about on the steps, in an ecstasy of sadistic pleasure. He looked around to his courtiers for approbation. "That is the most artistic thing I ever conceived! Don't you see, he's playing his own funeral music—on the bell which stands for the liberty his country is losing! Isn't it perfect?"

Down in the street, Diane, with Bledsoe at her side, stood looking up at the swinging, twitching figure on the bell, straining at the cords which bound her wrists, unable to tear her eyes from the awful sight. The heads of everybody present were craning upward, fascinated by the sight. But Diane Elliot alone knew indescribable agony of soul. Unashamedly, she let tears fill her eyes, drip saltily to her lips.

"Jimmy!" she said hoarsely, in a whisper. "Jimmy! It—it— can't be!"

The bell was booming now in swift cadence as it swung more swiftly. The human knocker had ceased to twitch, but the metal on his heels brought sound each time they struck the sides. His head hung at a queer angle, and his neck seemed inches longer than it had been before. A deep sigh arose from the populace. They knew that he was dead.

And Diane's lips were trembling. She was sagging, would have fallen had not a guard supported her. Bledsoe, looking at her, closed his eyes, murmured: "God! If she only loved me that way!"

THE BELL ceased to boom. They had slowed it up, brought it to a stop. A soldier brought a ladder, climbed up and cut the hemp above the noose. The dead body thumped to the ground, the iron mask clanged against the pavement, and the body lay still, the head twisted around grotesquely.

They lifted him, carried him over to the steps, laid him at the feet of Rudolph. There was a vast hush over the assemblage in the street as they realized that the mask was about to be removed. They would know now upon whom the conqueror had visited this gruesome death.

Rudolph swung to Anita. "Now, cousin," his eyes were shining craftily, "you shall see your hero's face. At least, now I shan't worry about your falling in love with him." He looked around. "Where is Hauglein? I want the combination to this mask!"

An officer stepped forward. "The count has not yet come, sire, but here is the Yankee, General Redfern, who also knows the combination."

Redfern stepped out from among the group behind the

emperor, and bowed low. A hiss went up from the crowd in the street. Redfern's face grew purple. Rudolph saw it, jeered: "They don't like you, do they, Redfern?"

The general's cheeks were haggard. "They think I betrayed them, your majesty. They don't know yet that I acted for their own good."

"All right. I can use you. I want an American like you who is not too well liked by his own people. You shall act as Hauglein's assistant in governing the country. But now—I want that mask opened. I want to show all these people that their last leader is gone. You know the combination?"

Redfern bowed, and bent, with trembling fingers spun the small dial, clicked open the lock. His hands shook so that he could not open the two halves of the mask which concealed the dead man's face. Rudolph eagerly pushed him aside, reached down with his own imperial hands and pulled the mask apart. Then he froze on his knee, gaping, with lower jaw hanging open. He uttered a shriek of rage. He was gazing into the purple, bloated features of Count Leopold von Hauglein!

CHAPTER 5
"WHO IS HE—THAT MADMAN?"

THE AUTOMOBILE road crossed a wide plain, lying straight as an arrow across the sun-scorched land. Far ahead it could be seen to enter a valley and then to disappear at a point near the horizon where the two mountains on either side seemed to converge upon it.

The air on the plain was still with the foreboding of doom. The only noise came from the Ford that labored with steaming radiator toward the sanctuary of those two mountains. Of the four men in the car, the driver was the only one who did not constantly look back toward the rolling hills behind them over which they had come. Accurately speaking, they were three men and a boy.

Jimmy Christopher was driving, and he kept both hands on the wheel, his eyes narrowed against the white-hot sun-glare that glanced off the burning road to drive through the wind-shield in blinding flashes. Beside him sat Tim Donovan, while Slips McGuire and Sergeant Geffen occupied the rear seat. The speedometer needle of the Ford kept around the seventy mark at all times.

Jimmy Christopher said to Tim Donovan, without taking his gaze off the road: "I still don't understand it, Tim. Diane was supposed to deliver the duplicate key that you had made, to von Hauglein, so that he wouldn't grow suspicious and come to the jail. Then she and Bledsoe were to drive out on the road and wait for us two miles outside of Topeka. Is that right?"

Tim nodded. "That's the way it was planned. She and Bled-soe were to time their arrival at the City Hall at the exact moment we cut the telephone wires, so the count wouldn't be able to phone the jail. Then she was supposed to try to delay von Hauglein with some excuse, in case he wanted to go right over. But the count surprised us by appearing when he did, so we just put the mask on him, and Slips and Geffen put on the two soldiers' uniforms and we turned him over to the Central Empire troops."

"Of course. I know that," Jimmy Christopher said impatiently. "Rudolph will probably go raving mad when he discovers who the Man in the Iron Mask is. But the point is, where's Diane? We waited at Topeka up to the last minute. We only left when we saw the Central Empire advance guard approaching. All the other fugitives passed us while we waited. And Diane wasn't among them. Maybe something went wrong with her plan, and she and this Lieutenant Bledsoe were held by Hauglein. It's too bad we couldn't question him before we gagged him. But if Diane is in that fiend Rudolph's hands—"

Slips McGuire interrupted caustically from the rear: "I suppose you'd want to go back and find her, huh?"

Jimmy nodded, without turning.

"Well," Slips went on, "you can't, see? You can't go back. You got to go on. And if you want to see for yourself, just take a look behind!"

Jimmy slowed up, turned and looked through the rear window. There, far behind them on the road, was a swirling cloud of dust. He pulled up at the side of the road, got out for a better look. "The radiator needs a chance to cool off, anyway," he said. The other got out too, stood there looking at the road behind. Presently they were able to make out moving trucks racing toward them. There were gray-clad, steel-helmeted troops in those trucks—the first divisions of the army of Emperor Rudolph, moving on toward Denver. High above those trucks, appearing suddenly out of the clouds in the distance, they glimpsed a flight of planes, saw the emblem of the severed head and the crossed broadswords on each.

Jimmy nodded morosely. "They're coming too fast for us. We've got to get far enough ahead of them to organize some resistance. Let's get going!"

He climbed into the car again, waited for the others, then started the motor and headed west again.

Sergeant Geffen, looking through the rear window, said anxiously: "Do you think those planes will bomb us or something? They'll be passing right over us in a minute."

"Why should they bomb us?" Jimmy asked bitterly. "Theoretically, there's no more resistance. They're merely advancing to take over a country that has officially surrendered!"

"Those guys are funny," Geffen said doubtfully. "They are liable to shoot you up just for the fun of it."

The planes were winging low over the road now. They had caught up with the Ford, and their shadows from the noontime sun fell directly in the path of the car. Jimmy Christopher kept the wheel steady, his foot pressed down on the accelerator.

TIM DONOVAN, peering upward out of his window, said: "They seem to be interested in us, Jimmy. I think we're in for it!"

As he spoke, the leading plane dipped, flew screaming across the road right in the path of the car. It skimmed by, rose again. But the pilot of that plane had put out his hand, palm out, in the familiar gesture of the stop signal. Undoubtedly he meant for the car to pull up.

Jimmy Christopher set his lips grimly, and kept his foot down on the gas. The plane rose high, came down once more in a power dive, from behind. Suddenly the road just ahead of the car began to look as if it were being peppered with little pellets. Only these weren't pellets. They were small grooves dug into the concrete by machine gun slugs.

Tim Donovan exclaimed: "He's warning us, Jimmy. We've got to stop, or the next burst will mean business!"

The plane rose again, looped and came back to fly above them and a little to the left. The pilot, leaning over, motioned with his gloved hand. Slips, from the rear seat, said: "You better stop, Jimmy. He's got us cold!"

Jimmy shrugged, slowed down, and pulled over to the side of the road. The plane screamed past them, almost brushing their top, and landed on the road more than two hundred yards ahead of them. The pilot jumped out, waved to them to drive up. The other planes were apparently leaving this matter to the single one that had landed, for they flew off in different directions, no doubt to observe the other roads in the neighborhood.

Jimmy started the car again, drove toward the waiting plane. There were two more men in that plane. "It's one of those new three-place Sigismund V216's that the Central Empire's using now," he explained to the others. "In addition to the pilot, it has accommodations for a man to manipulate the bombing device, and for a man in the rear to operate the stern machine guns. You'll notice it has machine guns fore and aft."

Indeed, there was a man in the rear cockpit, sighting with a machine gun directly at them, while the pilot stood to one side. When the car was within fifty feet of the plane, the pilot in the road put up a hand, motioning for them to stop.

Tim Donovan said: "Jimmy, I don't like it. Those birds look mean."

Geffen, in the back, guffawed. "You'll take it and like it, kid. With a machine gun looking down your gullet, you'll like it!"

Jimmy Christopher pushed open the door of the car, stepped out on the road. The pilot called out in guttural English: "Raise your hands in the air! We wish to question you. You will not be harmed if you are not the man we seek!"

Jimmy raised his hands. Out of the corner of his mouth he said to Tim: "Got a gun, Timmy?"

"Right, Jimmy. I have one in my hand."

"All right, hold it."

The pilot was saying: "We are looking for a fugitive who is known as Operator 5, who escaped from Kansas City yesterday. Each of you in turn will come forward and show your credentials. You—" he pointed at Jimmy—"first. Then you will go back to the car, and the next man will come out."

Jimmy did not move forward. He kept his hands up, his eyes on the machine gunner in the rear cockpit of the plane. He noted that the gunner was watching the car closely. At the first sign of a gun or pistol being poked out of a window, he would spray the Ford. There would be no chance of Geffen or Tim or Slips shooting him from the car. To do so would invite their instant death. Yet Jimmy knew that they would not allow him or themselves to be captured without putting up a fight. And they would surely be held when they failed to show proper identification.

Instead of walking forward in obedience to the pilot's

command, Jimmy called out: "I'll have to get my papers out of the car. I haven't got them with me."

A gun appeared in the pilot's hand. "All right. Reach in and get them. But no tricks."

Jimmy turned, leaned into the car, pretended to fumble with papers in the glove compartment on the dashboard. "Give me the gun, Tim!" he ordered.

Tim, white-faced, handed over the automatic he had been holding. Jimmy stepped away from the car, holding the automatic out at arm's length. The pilot uttered an excited shout, raised his own gun, and the man in the plane swiveled the machine gun toward Jimmy, shouting to the pilot: "Stand away, Kurt!"

Operator 5's automatic spoke twice in quick succession. His first shot caught the machine gunner in the head, sprayed the man's brains over the cockpit.

The pilot, instead of shooting, had stepped aside out of the path of the machine gun. Now, Jimmy's second shot caught him between the eyes, and he staggered backward, sprawled on his back in the road, dead.

Jimmy Christopher leaped forward, crouching. There might be a third man in the center cockpit. But there was none. This plane had gone up with only two men, doubtless because they expected to do only reconnoitering, and no fighting.

Tim, Geffen and Slips McGuire came charging out of the Ford, and Geffen boomed: "Say, that was the swellest piece of shootin' I seen in my whole life! Zowie! Right where it counted—both times!"

OPERATOR 5 was already kneeling beside the dead pilot, stripping his helmet and uniform from him. He rapped out crisply: "Hurry, you fellows. Strip the uniform off the observer, too. We may need them. And load both the bodies into the Ford. We're commandeering the plane!"

For a moment the three of them stared at him, open-mouthed. Then Tim exclaimed: "Boy-o-boy! What a guy! Let's get going!"

In a trice the two stripped Central Empire officers were loaded into the Ford, and Jimmy was in the pilot's pit. Geffen took the middle, and Slips the rear seat, with Tim Donovan strapped on his lap. The other planes were far off to the west, over the mountains toward which the Ford had been heading. They had noticed nothing of what was going on.

Jimmy Christopher felt the controls of the plane lovingly. "This is a beauty!" he shouted back to the others above the roar of the two powerful engines. "If we had a thousand like these we could push Rudolph back to the Atlantic. No wonder they blasted our air force out of the air in two days with equipment like this!"

The road afforded a perfect take-off field, and in a moment he had the big crate up in the air, heading west. Looking back, he could see the long column down below, of the Central Empire troops, debouching into the road from the hills. There were two

In one spot the whole countryside seemed to rise up in the air—an ammunition train had been hit!

long lines of trucks, heavy caissons, and long ribbons of marching men.

Geffen tapped him on the shoulder, cupped his hands, and shouted: "Let's go back and strafe those fellows. There's ten bombs slung underneath here. And I think I can work these levers!"

Jimmy Christopher's eyes were glinting with the light of battle. He nodded, banked around and headed back along the road toward the moving column. The idea of attacking the marching troops of the Central Empire was not a wild gesture. Operator 5's keen mind had immediately grasped the desirability of such a move. While Sergeant Geffen thought of it only as daring, reckless thing to do, Jimmy Christopher had a deeper purpose. At present, America was licked. There might be sporadic outbursts of isolated rebellion against the conquerors; but the country as a whole would be under the heel of Rudolph from coast to coast within another day or two. Without the leadership of the General Staff and with the Army of the Mississippi disbanded, the easiest thing would be to submit. The Central Empire would take over complete control without opposition. But if Rudolph's troops could be incensed to the point where they should advance with fire and sword instead of with the scaffold and the chopping block, Americans would be forced to resist.

None of the three guessed what was in his mind when he hurled the huge Sigismund at the head of that advancing column. The leading trucks of the Central Empire advance guard consisted of a company of engineers. Behind them was a field artillery battery, and behind the battery were masses of infantry. Jimmy chose the artillery caissons. He adjusted the earphones at his elbow, pressed the button connecting him with Geffen's cockpit, and said crisply:

"When I raise my hand, drop the first bomb, Geffen. Not before. Understand?"

"Okay, sir!" the sergeant replied joyfully.

Jimmy pushed the stick forward, catapulted down, until the leading truck was in the sights of the double machine guns mounted on the front cockpit. He pulled the trip and a fiery line of tracers stung through the air at the trucks. But he was careful to shoot just high enough so that the first burst went over the heads of the men in the truck. He wanted to give them a sporting chance.

He passed low over the truck, pulled up, banked around and rose. He looked down, grinning, to see that his unexpected action had disrupted the whole enemy line. They had, of course, not known the plane was in alien hands, and they had not expected to be fired upon by their own airmen. Dozens of small figures were scurrying away from the leading trucks, running out into the fields, looking up in amazement and terror at the plane. The column had halted abruptly, and the troops way down the line were jammed up against those ahead. Officers were waving angrily in the air. Far to the west the rest of the flight was flying high, oblivious of what was going on behind them.

Jimmy saw that the trucks were entirely deserted by the engineers, and that the men in the field battery had also left the road. He gauged his position accurately, raised his hand just before the plane passed over the battery, allowing for drift and for wind velocity. Behind him, Geffen pulled a lever. Jimmy pulled the plane up sharply, then leveled off and looked down just as a terrific detonation down below set cross-currents of wind eddying about the plane.

DOWN THERE on the road, there was a huge black ball of smoke where the field battery had been. The smoke cleared a little, revealing the torn-up road and bits of wreckage of caissons and guns. Jimmy glanced back to see Geffen grinning broadly, and Tim Donovan, in the last seat with Slips McGuire, hugging himself in glee. The first bomb had been a bull's-eye.

Operator 5 swung the plane back again, onto the road, and raced east above the now panic-stricken column, raising his hand at intervals in signal to Geffen to release more bombs. In five minutes he covered ten miles and they dropped their entire load. Detonation followed detonation, and in one spot the whole countryside seemed to rise up into the air. A lucky hit had struck an ammunition train! In a matter of five minutes incalculable destruction had been inflicted and the entire column was demoralized by a single plane! Of course, the element of surprise favored the daring maneuver. Now, Jimmy saw several trucks racing down the road from the east, with the long snouts of anti-aircraft guns pointing skyward. Soon the Central Empire army would be ready to retaliate. It was time to move on. And besides, there were no more bombs.

Operator 5 glanced toward the west, saw the rest of the flight of planes racing toward them. On his dashboard a bulb glowed, and Jimmy knew it was the radio signal. The ground forces

wished to communicate with him. They had no doubt been calling all the time that the column was being *strafed*, but Jimmy
was too busy to notice it. Now he experimented with some of
the buttons of the dash, and finally caught an excited, guttural
voice in the earphones. Some one was saying in the language of
the Central Empire:

"Gott! He is a madman! He has gone insane. He bombs our
troops. Captain Honig, he is someone from your flight. Fly back
at once and shoot him down. He is insane! Who is he?"

Jimmy Christopher laughed, sent the plane into a vertical
bank that carried it high above the swiftly approaching flight
of enemy craft, as well as out of the lanes of anti-craft fire that
were beginning to sizzle upward from the hastily set up battery.

He disconnected the ground radio, swung in the inter-cock-
pit telephone, and said: 'Well, boys, we gave them hell. Now we
have to try to get out of this. Slips, see to your machine guns.
It's going to be a stern chase!"

Slips replied cheerfully: "Let 'em come, Jimmy. After what
we just gave 'em, I don't care if we do go down!"

Jimmy Christopher gave the plane everything she would
take. Wind shrieked in the struts, and the vibration of the wings
seemed to warn that the plane would fall apart any moment. But
Jimmy kept her at that speed, angling downward directly at the
approaching flight of enemy ships. As he hurtled down upon
them at a hundred and seventy miles an hour, the enemy flight
split before him, and he sailed through them, zooming upward
while they were still maneuvering to come on his tail.

Behind, McGuire's machine guns began to chatter insistently.

After a moment McGuire shouted: "We've left 'em behind, Jimmy. They're out of range!"

The plane was clearing the top of the mountain at the western end of the road. The enemy pursuit was still after them, but they had a good start, and the distance between them was considerable. Geffen spoke into his telephone: "I guess it's a clean getaway, Operator 5. They'll never catch us now!"

Jimmy clicked on the ground communication once more, heard the ground officer talking to the flight commander: "*Himmel!* You have let him escape! He has destroyed our whole advance guard! Captain Honig, you shall be held personally responsible for this! Who is that madman?"

Jimmy chuckled, spoke into the transmitter: "I am no madman, sir. I inform you that you have had the honor to be strafed by Operator 5. Come and see us sometime. We'll have a nice reception ready for you!"

And he clicked off the connection, flew serenely westward.

CHAPTER 6
"DEAD MAN'S BATTALION"

FAR AHEAD, a cluster of little specks down on the ground indicated a town. Jimmy Christopher pointed to it. "We'll land there," he told Geffen and the others. "Our gas is low. That must be one of the reasons why those planes didn't stay on our tail."

Behind them, they were cut off from view of the Central Empire column by the mountains over which they had flown.

Below, the black road lay empty and untraveled, leading to the town where it was bisected at an angle by another road which led northeast. Far to the north they could see the glinting water of the Platte River, reflecting the glare of the sun. The bisecting road ran up toward the Platte, and in the distance, where it met the river, they could see another town.

Jimmy consulted the map which hung in a convenient bracket at his elbow, then pointed ahead, told the others: "That town must be Windsor. The one to the north is probably Framington."

He came down low, circled the town, peering over the side. The others were also inspecting it, and Geffen said: "It's deserted. I don't see a soul."

Tim called from the rear: "I see a couple of gas stations. Maybe we can dig up some gas."

Jimmy nodded, pointed the nose of the plane down against the wind and made a perfect landing on the road between two buildings. The building on the left was a two story frame structure with the name "Windsor Hotel" in gilt letters on a black sign over the entrance. The one on the right was a small stone affair with grilled windows. Chiseled into the stone at the side of the doorway was the information that this was the Windsor police department. Beyond the police station was a large garage with wide rolling doors which were closed. The town sprawled on from there, with a couple of factory buildings and a double row of stores along the highway, called Main Street. But there wasn't a sign of life in the entire town.

Jimmy climbed out of the cockpit. Geffen, Tim and Slips joined him. The big plane filled the road with its immense wing spread, and they had to pass under the wings with their hideous emblems of the crossed broadswords and the severed head. Tim Donovan was having the time of his life. He did a handspring on the hot pavement, came to his feet and gazed down the deserted street of the town.

His face lengthened. "Gee, Jimmy," he exclaimed, "this is like a ghost town. Everybody gone from it! You'd think there'd been a pestilence here!"

Jimmy Christopher was looking around keenly. That marvelous sixth sense of his, which sometimes appeared to be almost psychic, told him that there was something wrong. He whispered to the others:

"Keep your hands on your guns. I don't think this place is as deserted as it looks. If we're cornered, we'll have to shoot it out. There isn't enough gas in the buggy to take off with."

Almost as if his words had been an awaited cue, the door of the Windsor Hotel began to open slowly, cautiously. Tim, who saw it first, kicked Jimmy's ankle, muttered out of the side of his mouth: "Pipe the hotel, Jimmy!"

The lad's hand stole out of his pocket with the heavy service revolver that he had taken from the body of one of the two Central Empire airmen and he held it close to his side, pointing toward the door.

Jimmy Christopher already had his own gun out, while Geffen and Slips drew theirs. Jimmy said curtly: "Slips and Geffen—watch the station house. Tim and I will take the hotel. Back to back—the four of us!"

Suddenly the door of the hotel was pushed wide open. A

stocky, middle aged man in a pair of overalls over an undershirt stood in the doorway, a long, twenty-two rifle in the crook of his arm. His finger was curled around the trigger. Behind him, Jimmy could see more men, could see various weapons, among them a sawed-off shotgun and a pitchfork.

The two groups faced each other, tensely. And then, abruptly, Operator 5 lowered his revolver and began to laugh. The stocky man frowned, did not relax his vigilance, but asked:

"Who be ye, strangers? Ye don't look like varmints from the Central Empire. How come ye to be in that plane?"

Jimmy called out: "You can put that gun down. We're friends. We took this plane away from a couple of Rudolph's tin soldiers!"

The other was still suspicious. So were the men crowding at his back inside the hotel. They shouted: "Look out, Hank! It sounds like a trick. They're aimin' to git us out in the open!"

Hank scowled. "If so be, you fellers are playin' a trick onto us...."

"Forget it!" Jimmy broke in impatiently. "I am Operator 5. We escaped from Kansas City."

"Operator 5!" Hank almost whispered the name. "I heerd you'd been kilt!"

"No, I wasn't killed. Will you put that gun down and come out here? What do you fellows think you're doing, holing up in a wooden shanty like that?"

"Why shouldn't we? We're a'goin' to give a good account of ourself when them Central Empire varmints come along. We'll shoot 'em to smithereens!"

JIMMY GROANED. "Don't you know that the machine

101

guns on those planes could make a sieve of that hotel? And a single shell could blow you to the middle of next week!"

Hank was dubious. "If you are Operator 5, then you ought to know the wounded feller we got in here. Come on in—but don't you or your pals try no tricks!"

Jimmy shrugged, pocketed his gun, and motioned to Tim and the others to wait for him. He walked up the steps of the hotel. Hank stood aside, looking him over curiously. The other men in the hotel made a lane for Jimmy to pass through. Jimmy saw that these were all older men, men who had not been at the front. He looked back into the street, saw that the door of the police station opposite had also opened, and that another group of men was peering out of there.

Hank called across: "I reckon these here fellers is all right. But just wait a few seconds while I test this here feller out."

He turned, shuffled in, and said to Jimmy: "Foller me, feller."

Operator 5 followed him up a broad flight of wooden stairs, to the second floor. The building was full of overalled and denim-clad men armed with weapons of every description, from modern rifles to woodsmen's axes. They all looked at him curiously, but stood out of the way respectfully when Hank motioned them aside.

Near the head of the stairs, Jimmy said: "Good God, man, were you going to make a stand here against the Central Empire army?"

Hank nodded brightly. "That was the idea. But this here wounded feller that we got in here, he says the same thing like you say. He says we couldn't hold this hotel nohow."

102

He led Jimmy into one of the rooms along the hall. The shades were drawn here, and a doctor sat at the side of the bed, upon which lay an emaciated, black-haired man, whose gaunt, hollow cheeks formed a fitting framework for the black, piercing eyes that stared out at Jimmy.

Operator 5 felt a quick pang at sight of that familiar face. "Z-7!" he exclaimed. His eyes traveled down to the wide, white bandage which swathed the wounded man's chest, and which was taped tight from under his armpits to his thighs. He knew that man well. Z-7 was the man who had been Jimmy Christopher's immediate superior in the Intelligence Service.* He had

---

* AUTHOR'S NOTE: Regular readers of these stories have met Z-7 often in the past. They are familiar with him as the indomitable leader of the entire United States Intelligence Service, not only in this country, but throughout the world. It was Z-7 who brought our own counter-espionage system to the state of perfection it had attained at the time of the invasion of the Central Empire. And it was not Z-7's fault, nor the fault of the Intelligence System which he headed, that America was unprepared for the cataclysm. There were on file in musty drawers in Washington, before the capital was destroyed by Rudolph, countless reports from Z-7 detailing the deadly improvements and discoveries of the militaristic nations of Europe. There was little in the way of scientific implements of destruction which Z-7 did not have full information about. In fact it will be noted by future historians that eleven months before the first gray-clad trooper of the Central Empire set foot within our country, Z-7 had filed a complete report of the number, types and equipment of the air force of the Central Empire, and that he had recommended increasing our own air force with modern ships of the

been operating on the West Coast, engaged in recruiting men for service on the Mississippi, and Operator 5 had not heard from him for a week prior to the surrender of Kansas City.

Z-7's wan face lit in a smile at sight of Operator 5. "Jimmy!" he said in a weak voice that barely carried across the room. "Jimmy! Thank God you're alive. I was beginning to think that that they'd really got you this time!"

The doctor bent over him, murmured: "Be careful, sir. Your ribs—"

But Z-7 waved him aside impatiently. "To hell with the ribs! Let me talk to this man!"

Jimmy Christopher rushed across the room and took the hand which Z-7 weakly extended. In the silent handclasp between these two men there was more expression of mutual esteem than might have been found in a multitude of words. The physician stood by, silent, while the man, Hank, watched them curiously, his rifle hanging loosely in his hand, the muzzle trailing the floor.

latest design. This recommendation, however, never saw the light of day for the reason that a wave of pacifist propaganda was sweeping the country at the time. If Z-7's recommendations had been followed, we would have been able to meet the Central Empire in the air on a basis of equality, and the war might have taken a different turn. Z-7 has always doggedly supported Operator 5 in the latter's unorthodox undertakings when the fate of the nation has been at stake. And only a few weeks ago, Z-7 faced a court-martial for Jimmy Christopher's sake. The bond of affection between these two may, therefore, be readily appreciated.

"Chief!" Jimmy said finally. "What happened to you? I didn't know you were at the Front!"

THOUGH OPERATOR 5 had been elevated by presidential decree to the post of high command of the armed forces of the United States, it was eloquent of his own character, as well as that of Z-7, that he still addressed this man as Chief.

Z-7 smiled bitterly. "I didn't get this at the front. I was in Los Angeles with Nan* when I heard that you had disappeared. There were rumors you had been captured, that the army was without leadership, and that the general staff was considering surrender. So I left your sister in charge of recruiting on the coast and flew to Denver. We had a crack-up when we landed, and I busted a couple of ribs. They wanted to put me in a base hospital, but I made them drive me to the Front. I thought I might be of some use in finding you. When we got here word came through that the general staff had surrendered, and that the

---

* AUTHOR'S NOTE: It is to be regretted that we will not meet Jimmy's twin sister, Nan Christopher, in this story. But Z-7's reference to her furnishes the occasion for a few words of introduction. It was this vivacious young lady, the exact counterpart of Operator 5—except for a certain elfin delicacy which only a girl can possess—who, in the early days of the invasion, held the powerhouse at Bellevue with only a handful of men against the armed forces of Rudolph, equipped with all the modern weapons of war. While all of New York City was in the hands of the invader, Jimmy Christopher arrived to rescue them. For a long time now, she, together with Tim Donovan, Diane Elliot and Slips McGuire, has shared notably in Operator 5's constant battle for the safety of his country.

trenches along the Mississippi were being evacuated. I couldn't get anybody to drive me further, so here I am!"

Jimmy grinned affectionately at Z-7. He was about to speak when the man, Hank, stepped forward. There was a new look of respect in the glance he gave Jimmy Christopher. "I guess if Z-7 says you're Operator 5, you must be Operator 5. But we sure thought you was dead. We was goin' to keep on fighting just the same, general staff or no general staff. There's plenty men in this neck of the woods that would ruther be killed fightin' than get their throats hacked in two on the block."

Jimmy glanced at Z-7, then said to Hank: "It's all right to fight, but what's the use of committing suicide? You've chosen just about the worst place in the world to defend against Rudolph's army. They're on the other side of the mountain now. When they come through the pass they'll just set up a battery and blow this whole town off the map!"

Hank looked a little bewildered. "I guess you're right, but we couldn't think of nothin' better to do. Now that you're here, why don't you take charge? They's some more of the boys over at Framington, holed in over there. An' we've been in touch with small bands of men all through Nebraska and the Dakotas who'd be glad to take orders from you." He suddenly became pathetically eager. "I bet you could organize a hell of a big army once the boys found out you was alive an' kickin'. What do you say, Operator 5?"

Jimmy asked him abruptly: "What's your name?"

"I'm Hank Sheridan—the mayor of Windsor," he said proudly, "Been mayor eleven times, an' they know all through this here part of the country. I don't aim to see no furriners lordin' it over us. Come on, Operator 5, we need you!"

For a moment, Jimmy glanced at Z-7, who nodded approvingly. "Go ahead, Jimmy. It's as good a place to start as any, and you won't find better fighters anywhere."

"I was thinking," Jimmy said slowly, "that I might only lead these men to their death. They are not equipped with modern arms; they have no facilities for digging trenches, and there is no coördinated food supply. The chances would be ten thousand to one against them, and I'd be responsible for their deaths."

Hank Sheridan interrupted him, snorting: "Huh! Don't you worry none about us gettin' killed. Looka here, Operator 5— you found us in this here town waitin' for Rudolph's army to come an' wipe us out. You say yourself that we wouldn't stand no chance here. All right, consider us dead. We'll be the Dead Man's Battalion. Our lives is forfeit already. We'll obey you till we're all kilt. Every one o' the boys feels like I do, an' if any says otherwise, I'll push his face in!"

JIMMY SUDDENLY smiled. "All right, Hank Sheridan! We'll form the Dead Man's Battalion. We'll fight Rudolph with whatever weapons we can find, and we'll keep on fighting till the end. Rudolph will know he's had a scrap, even if he does win!"

Hank let out a whoop. "Wait'll I tell the boys! We got a radio hook-up, an' we been talkin' to about thutty groups of boys all over this an' surroundin' states. Well notify 'em all to hold theirselves subject to your orders!"

He started for the door in a burst of enthusiasm.

"Wait!" said Jimmy. Hank stopped, looked at him questioningly.

"How many men have you got here in Windsor?"

"About three hundred. There's a hundred or so of the men from the village, and the rest is doughboys who stopped off on the way from the trenches. They quit when the general staff surrendered. They started back for their homes, but when they saw we was determined to stick here, they figgered they'd stay with us."

"How many of the men have rifles?"

"I figger about two hundred. An' there's three machine guns that the doughboys brung with them. We got one mounted in the upper floor of the station house, one in the front window here in the hotel, an' one in the garage."

Jimmy Christopher said thoughtfully: "Two hundred rifles and three machine guns, eh? That would be enough to stand off an army for a long time—in the right place."

"An' where's the right place?" Hank asked.

Jimmy's eyes were gleaming. "Don't you see it, Hank? That pass back there, between the two mountains!"

"You mean Snyder pass! Sure! Why didn't I think of that myself? Lord, we could take positions on both sides. There's plenty o' cover there—an' we could pick 'em off as they come through. Why, we could keep 'em out forever!"

Jimmy shook his head. "Not forever, Hank. You forget that they have planes that can drop gas bombs. They'd get you pretty soon. But if we ambushed them, we could do plenty of damage before they got us. If we only had a couple of anti-aircraft guns—"

Z-7 stirred in his bed, spoke weakly: "Jimmy! You could take care of the planes! There's General Stover's anti-aircraft battalion. A whole battalion of anti-aircraft guns—loaded on flat cars on the railroad near Silvertown. They were to be distributed along the front. When word came of the surrender, they were abandoned. The railroad isn't running—the crews have all quit—but if we could get those guns moving—" He struggled to a sitting position, motioned to the physician. "Get me dressed, doctor! I'm going to take care of that end of it!"

The doctor protested. "But you aren't fit to be up, sir. Your injury—"

Z-7 glared at him. "The devil with that! Get me dressed, I tell you!"

Jimmy Christopher's eyes were warm. He nodded to the doctor. "Do as he says. Z-7 is the only man who can bring those guns up here. And with them, we can do more than just give Rudolph a scrap—we may be able to turn the tide of history!"

He was already helping Z-7 to his feet. "Do you think you can make it, Chief?"

"Do I think I can make it!" Z-7 laughed harshly. "I can make a damn good try. I'd rather do that than lie here and wait to be taken prisoner by Rudolph!"

He was on his feet now, and though he was pale, he managed to stand firmly, with his shoulders back. He twinged with pain as he took a step. "You have a plane out there. Get Tim to fly me to Silvertown. I'll commandeer trucks and have those guns here inside of two hours—if you can hold out that long!"

Jimmy looked at Hank. "Is there any gas in this town?"

Hank Sheridan nodded. "We got two Standard Oil trucks full. They're parked in back of town."

"All right. Tell some of the boys to drive one over here. We'll gas up the plane." Jimmy faced Z-7, shook hands with him. "Good luck, Z-7. If you get to those guns, send some here and stay with the rest. I'm going to try to organize more groups like this one, and post them at strategic spots all along the front of Rudolph's advance. We'll get in touch with those boys Hank was talking about."

He stopped as Hank called to him excitedly from the window: "Operator 5! Come here, quick! Gawd, look at that!"

JIMMY HURRIED over to the window. Downstairs in

Marshal Kremer   Anita Monfred

Emperor Rudolph

front of the hotel Tim, Slips and Geffen were standing with a group of the men from the town, all gathered about the plane. They were staring up toward the north, in the direction in which Hank was pointing. Jimmy Christopher's lips tightened. For there, in the sky, was a patrol of five Central Empire planes. It was not the same patrol they had met on the other side of the mountain—these ships were coming from the north. But they were heading in a direction which would carry them right over the town, and it was certain that they would spot the big plane on the road.

"Gawd!" Hank exclaimed again. "They'll bomb us! They'll wipe us out afore we can get started!"

Jimmy gripped him by the shoulder, pushed him away from the window and leaned out. Tim was looking up toward the window. Men were streaming out of the station house and the garage, from the lower floor of the hotel, scattering down the road to take up positions with their rifles. The flight of enemy planes was winging swiftly toward them, and they had not yet spotted the plane in the road, there was no way to hide it. The enemy would surely come lower to investigate when they saw one of their own ships in the road.

Z-7 had come up beside Jimmy. He said: "Jimmy! Those men are brave, but they can't fight a squadron of planes with rifles. A couple of bombs will wipe out the whole town—"

Jimmy nodded. He swung from the window, seized Sheridan by the elbow, spoke quickly. "Hank, you tell those boys of yours to get under cover fast. Understand?"

"But golly, Operator 5, when the planes see your ship there, they'll want to know about it!"

"Of course they will. And I've got a plan. Now quick! Do as I say!"

Hank said: "Okay, Operator 5. I said I'd take orders from you, and by golly, I will!" He poked his head out of the window.

"All you fellers get back under cover!" he shouted. "Don't show yourselves. Make it snappy!"

The men looked up at him and one or two started to protest, but he squelched them. In a moment they were streaming back toward their shelter in the station house and the garage.

Jimmy called down: "Tim! Get those two uniforms out of the plane, and bring them up here. Geffen and Slips, come up too."

Tim Donovan nodded eagerly, ran to the plane and dug out the two uniforms they had taken from the Central Empire aviators. By now the street was cleared of defenders, and when Tim, Slips and Geffen entered the hotel, it presented the same appearance of desolation as when Jimmy had landed a short while ago. The enemy planes were close now, and Jimmy, hiding behind a curtain, peered out and saw that they were sweeping in a wide circle overhead.

Feverishly he began to tear his own clothes off, and when Tim entered with Slips and Geffen, he began to don one of the uniforms. "You, Geffen," he ordered, "get into the other one. We're going downstairs and show ourselves in these duds!"

Geffen eagerly began to strip, grinning broadly. "I get it," he said. "We make 'em think we're their pals, eh?" He ran his fore-finger across his throat in a suggestive gesture. "Some pals we'll turn out to be!"

Tim Donovan was shaking hands with Z-7 while Hank was watching the trick procedure uncomprehendingly. He hadn't yet grasped Jimmy's idea.

When Jimmy and Geffen were dressed they looked like typi-cal Central Empire officers. Geffen's broad face was spread in a

113

wide beam of pleasure as he stood stiffly to attention and saluted. Jimmy nodded approvingly. "You'll do, Geffen. If those boys come down"—he cast a glance toward the window, whence came the loud droning of the enemy planes flying low—"you just stand like that, and keep your mouth shut. I'll do the talking." He swung to Sheridan. "Hank! You post your boys at the window with rifles. They're not to show themselves under any circumstances, until I give the word. Understand?"

Hank shook his head. "I don't understand, but I'll do like you say, anyway."

Jimmy clapped him gaily on the back. "That's the spirit, Hank. Maybe we'll have an air force before we're through!"

He waved to Z-7 and Tim, motioned to Geffen to follow him, and then hurried downstairs under the amazed stares of the defenders of the hotel. Out in the street, Jimmy shaded his eyes, looked upward. The enemy flight was circling the town, and Jimmy could see the heads of the airmen peering over the sides.

He lifted an arm, waved to them, at the same time saying to Geffen: "I hope they come down to investigate before they report to headquarters about this plane. If they report first, headquarters will tell them about our strafing their column, and our stunt will be all off!"

He watched anxiously, and with relief saw the pilot of the leading plane waving back in response. A moment later the first plane left the formation, banked around into the wind, and came down toward the road. It taxied to a perfect stop just behind Jimmy's plane. The other four ships continued to circle the town.

Jimmy frowned. "Now," he said to Geffen, "comes the ticklish part of this business." He glanced up toward the first floor window of the hotel, caught a glimpse of Tim Donovan's freckled face peering out at him. He frowned, and the face disappeared. Then he started to walk toward the enemy plane, with Geffen just behind him.

CHAPTER 7
A MESSAGE OF DOOM!

THERE WERE three men in that plane. Apparently this patrol was carrying a full complement. Jimmy saw that the pilot, who had already climbed out, wore the uniform of a major of the Central Empire air force. Three gold bars gleamed on his sleeve under the emblem of the crossed broadswords and the severed head, which every Central Empire officer carried on his armband. Jimmy's own uniform carried two silver stripes which indicated the rank of lieutenant.

Jimmy came up within a few feet of the other, saluted stiffly in the manner of the Central Empire. The major returned his salute and spoke in his own guttural language. "You were forced down here, Lieutenant? You have some trouble?"

Jimmy answered him, speaking the foreign tongue fluently. "I landed here, Herr Major, but could not take off again for lack of petrol."

The major glanced at the numbers on the wings of Jimmy's plane. "H'm. You are of Captain Honig's Third Imperial Pursuit Squadron. They are attached to General Feld's column. Where are your fellow fliers?"

"They have gone back to the column, Herr Major. No doubt they will return soon with petrol." Jimmy glanced up at the other planes, circling the town, then at the major. "You are with another column—to the north, perhaps, sir?"

The other nodded. "I am Major von Sturm, commander of the First Division of the Imperial Flying Forces. But I have never seen you before, Lieutenant." He was eyeing Jimmy, not yet suspiciously, but with a queer look of interrogation. "I have made it a habit to meet all the men in my command personally, but I do not recall you or your observer."

"If you please, Herr Major," Jimmy broke in hurriedly, in order to forestall further questions, "I have used my time here to look around the town. And I have found something of great interest in this building." He pointed to the hotel. "If you would care to look at it—"

"Something of interest? What do you mean?"

"There is evidence in there, Herr Major, that this Operator 5 whom we seek is in the neighborhood."

"Operator 5? You don't say! Wonderful! If we can capture him the Emperor's gratitude will know no bounds! What is this?"

"If you will come inside, sir," Jimmy was already piloting the other toward the door of the hotel. He winked at Geffen, who stood aside for them to pass, then moved over so that he was facing the other two officers from the plane. These two had also gotten out, and Geffen watched them, with a hand on the revolver in his holster.

Major von Sturm threw back over his shoulder: "Come with us, Gerber and Krauss."

One of the two stepped forward, looking suspiciously at Jimmy, "Excuse me, Herr Major. But there is something strange here. I know this plane. It is one that has been used constantly by Lieutenant Stiegmanner, who is a good friend of mine. See, there is the number—C. E. 4242. I recall the number very well. Yet, here are these two strangers—"

Jimmy interrupted him quietly. "You are very observant, Lieutenant. It is too bad that you are so observant!" As if by magic there appeared in his hand the revolver from his holster. He held it inconspicuously, so that it would not be noticed from the air by the rest of the major's flight, who were still circling above. "Stand still!" he ordered. "I will shoot you at the first move!"

Geffen, who had not understood the conversation, but who had understood the action, stepped behind the major's two men and drew his own gun.

Jimmy said quickly: "Be careful, Geffen. Don't let those birds up in the air guess what's taking place!"

The two men stood still, under Geffen's gun. But the major, facing Jimmy, grew red in the face. "You swine!" he shouted. "You are not the emperor's man. I know who you are. You are Operator 5!" And von Sturm made a quick movement toward his own holster.

Jimmy's taut body swung into action with the smoothness of well-oiled, precision-fitted machinery. He stepped in close to the major, turned on his toes so that he was alongside him, his left side almost touching von Sturm's right. Jimmy slid the revolver into its holster once more. To use it would have been fatal, for the watching eyes of the airman in the crates above would have been sure to spot such a shooting. But what Jimmy did now could not have been noticed by the keenest eyes from the air.

WITH HIS right hand he seized von Sturm's forearm just below the elbow. With his left he reached around behind the major, and gripped von Sturm's left arm, just at the elbow. The long, powerful fingers of Jimmy's right hand held von Sturm's gun arm in an unshakeable grip. Jimmy pressed downward, and since von Sturm's finger was curled about the trigger of the gun in his holster, and his hand was wrapped around the butt, the major could only escape from that grip by lifting upward with his arm. This was impossible against the weight which Jimmy Christopher threw into the grip on the major's elbow. It was an application of the principles of jiu-jitsu—the pitting of the science of balance and leverage against bare strength. But it was a little more than that; it was opportunism, too. In the schools of Nippon, where Operator 5 had mastered all the intricacies of the "gentle art," * he learned that knowledge of jiu-jitsu is not a

---

* AUTHOR's NOTE: "Gentle art" is a literal translation of the word, jiu-jitsu. Although many of the orthodox holds and pressures of this art have become widely known throughout the Orient, there are a few lean and adventurous men here and there in odd spots of the world, who will tell you in a moment of confidence, that *all* the secrets of this mysterious science which were known to the Samurai of old Japan have not yet become public property. And the white races will never, perhaps, know everything that was known to the Samurai. Jimmy Christopher's knowledge was obtained under the tutelage of *Kashawatska Hoia,* the trainer of the emperor's bodyguard in Tokyo—and

trick in itself, but a broad general science which must be applied to the occasion as opportunity arises and demands. Thus, the lightning-quick reflexes of his mind had seen the weakness of von Sturm's physical position and had taken advantage. A boy weighing no more than a hundred pounds, with the same quick mental reactions, and with the same knowledge of the tremendous importance of leverage, could have held the major's arm in exactly the same grip.

In the meantime, Jimmy Christopher's left hand, behind the major's back, held von Sturm's left arm, while his fingers kneaded cruelly into the elbow. The major groaned with the sudden agony in his elbow, and sweat started to course down his face. Jimmy propelled him toward the door and, to the airmen looking down from the planes, it appeared that von Sturm had found a very good friend who was taking him into the hotel— so good a friend in fact, that he had his arm around him, and when the major stumbled on the steps, helped him up and into the doorway.

Once inside, Jimmy released his grip, hurled the major

how he qualified as a disciple of a story in itself. Suffice it for the present to say that Operator 5 is one of the *Fawa Ho*, which is the deadliest of all the tricks of jiu-jitsu, and which produces instant death. It is the trick which was thought to have perished from human knowledge at the time of the great resistance of the *Saigō of Satsuma*, in 1887, when the Samurai were almost annihilated. But it has survived. And those to whom it is imparted, together with other little known mysteries of the "gentle art," are under fearful oath to reveal it to none but the elect.

forward into the arms of the crowd of waiting men who had been watching the scene with avidity. They seized von Sturm, not yet recovered from the agony of the pain in his elbow, and held him helpless. Jimmy whirled toward the doorway, called out to the other two Central Empire officers who were standing transfixed with Geffen behind them:

"Come forward, you two, and enter. If you make a single move, your major will be killed instantly!"

Whether it was regard for their major or the fear of Geffen's gun, Jimmy didn't bother to discover. He only watched them, hawklike, while they came up the steps and entered the room. Geffen came in after them, shut the door, and bellowed: "Well, how was that? Did we do it, or didn't we do it?"

The two officers were quickly seized. Jimmy ordered crisply: "Take their uniforms off—quick! And give me the major's! We're not through yet. The job's just started!" He noticed Z-7, standing at the head of the stairs with Tim beside him, waved to them, then turned back to the business in hand.

He quickly stripped off his own lieutenant's tunic, put on that of the major. "Three of you men," he ordered, put on these uniforms. We're all going out again and make faces at the other planes!"

Hank Sheridan picked out two men who most nearly resembled in height the two officers of the Central Empire and another man to put on the uniform which Jimmy had discarded. In a few moments they were all dressed, and the half-clad figures of von Sturm and his two aides were trussed up and carted away.

Jimmy motioned to the uniformed men to follow him and, together, they went out into the sunshine again.

ALMOST SUBCONSCIOUSLY Jimmy Christopher assumed the bearing and stride of Major von Sturm. It was one of his great qualities, one of the things which had made him so successful in intelligence work. He could, at will, take on the attributes of any man whom he wished to impersonate, and he did it so wholeheartedly, so keenly, that he almost *thought* as the other man did. To anyone viewing him from the air he was without any doubt the same Major von Sturm who had entered the hotel only a few minutes ago.

The men in the four enemy planes were growing impatient. They were flying low, peering down at the road. The planes were directly overhead, and Jimmy Christopher could see the helmeted heads of the pilots and their observers. He raised his arm in a commanding gesture—just such a gesture as Major von Sturm would have used, lowered it in a sweeping arc, indicating that the other planes were to come down. The planes passed, banked around and came back. Jimmy repeated the gesture.

One of the airmen raised a hand in acknowledgment, and the four planes rose, came around into the wind over the road.

Jimmy's eyes were sparkling with excitement as he glanced behind him at Geffen and the two other boys in uniform. Then he looked up, caught sight of Hank Sheridan, Tom Donovan and Z-7 in the doorway of the hotel. Across the street, many of the men were peering from the windows of the police station and from the doorway of the garage, unable to restrain their curiosity at what was going to happen.

121

Jimmy called out to them: "Get your machine guns trained on that road, boys. And those with rifles take positions at every window that commands the road. When I give the word, open up—but not before. We want to do this without bloodshed if we can!"

Hank Sheridan, from the doorway of the hotel, called out: "Boys, you do jest like this feller says. He's Operator 5!"

There was a moment of silence following the announcement, and then a low cheer. Jimmy Christopher cut it short "On your toes, boys!" he commanded urgently. "The first plane is landing!"

One after another the four Central Empire planes with the dreaded insignia of the crossed broadswords and the severed head on their wings taxied down the road to a halt. There were now six planes in line. The eight men from the four planes which had just landed climbed out, and came toward the figure of the man they thought to be their major. Suddenly they stopped as the foremost of them got close enough to distinguish Jimmy's face. This one stood rooted to the ground in surprise, his hand creeping toward his gun. "Who are you?" he demanded hoarsely.

Jimmy Christopher smiled at him. "I am Operator 5. Do not draw your gun. You are covered by machine guns and rifles from every window in these buildings. It would be suicide for you to resist. I call upon you to surrender!"

The aviators were bewildered, uncertain. In the air, with the controls of a powerful ship under their hands and with the trips of synchronized, death-dealing machine guns ready to their touch, they were assured, domineering, masters of themselves. But on the ground, with only revolvers in their belts, and with the tables turned so that they now faced the deadly muzzles of machine guns, they were not the same men.

To clinch the situation, Jimmy Christopher raised his voice. "Show them it's not a bluff, boys. Show them where the slugs will come from!"

Immediately there was a loud shout of glee from three hundred throats, and faces appeared at every window. A shade in the upper floor of the hotel was ripped away, revealing the snout of a machine-gun pointing directly down at the unfortunate airmen. Another shade was raised in the station house and a second machine-gun appeared.

"You see," Jimmy Christopher said, smiling, "I speak nothing but the truth. The choice is yours—surrender, or a quick death." He shrugged. "It is immaterial to me which you choose. In fact, I think my men would rather practice a little shooting. They've been shot at for so long in the front lines, I think the change will do them good!"

The eight airmen were grouped closely together. They glanced at each other, spoke swiftly among themselves, and as Jimmy Christopher stirred impatiently, one of them shouted hastily: "We surrender. Don't shoot!" Jimmy bowed. "You spoke just in time. Drop your guns where you stand, and come forward. You will be treated honorably, as prisoners of war—better treatment than your emperor has accorded to his prisoners!"

As the Central Empire airmen let their weapons drop to the ground, Jimmy turned and waved gaily. "All right, boys. You can come out now!"

Immediately the street was filled with wildly howling men,

waving their weapons, shouting, and thronging about Jimmy Christopher to shake his hand and pat him on the back. The eight aviators were taken inside to join the major. Hank Sheridan came out, helping Z-7 to walk. Tim Donovan and Slips McGuire followed them.

Z-7 LOOKED at Jimmy, and there was moisture in his eyes. "You've done the impossible, Jimmy! You've captured a whole flight of enemy planes, intact, ready for use; and you did it without leaving the ground!"

"Now comes the hard part, Chief," Jimmy said. "You've got to take one of those planes, and fly back. Go to Silverton first, and get those anti-aircraft guns rolling. Then find me a dozen men who can fly these crates. Send them back by plane as fast as you can. We're going to have an air force on the front—and this is going to be the new front. We'll choose spots along every road by which Rudolph can advance—and we'll defend those spots with every weapon available till you can rush more men and more weapons to us!"

Z-7 seemed to be fired by the same enthusiasm that had seized Operator 5. For that matter, every man among them was changed since the planes had been captured. Up to now, they had constituted a stubborn, forlorn hope, willing to sell their lives as dearly as possible, with no expectation of stopping the mighty armies of the Central Empire. Now, however, that they had seen the impossible accomplished by this young man with the flashing eyes, they began to believe in miracles.

Hank Sheridan came up to him, asked: "What next, Operator 5? Say the word, and we'll march against the whole damned Central Empire!"

Jimmy smiled. "The next step is to hide those planes till we need them. Wheel them off the road, and cover them with tarpaulins, then throw leaves, grass over them—anything that will camouflage them."

"Right, sir!" Hank exclaimed. He detailed some fifty men for the task.

"Leave the first plane for Z-7 to take off in. Fill it up with gas," Jimmy continued. "And next, find as many automobiles in the town as you can. Get them ready to carry us toward that pass." He gestured toward the spot where the road wound in between the two mountains. "We're going to stop Rudolph right there. His column won't reach that pass for another hour or so—we disrupted it pretty badly with those bombs we dropped. Load the machine guns in the autos, and send them over there. Choose high spots along the sides of the road and set them up so that we can enfilade the column when it enters the pass."

Hank saluted awkwardly, and hurried away to carry out the orders, taking most of the men with him. A small group was left in front of the Hotel—Operator 5, Z-7, Tim Donovan and Slips McGuire. Tim Donovan clutched Jimmy's sleeve.

"Jimmy, I have some news for you."

Operator 5 tensed at the tone of the boy's voice. He glanced down sharply. "Yes?" he asked harshly.

The boy went on, his voice low. "There's a radio hooked up in the hotel. While you were out here, I sent out some calls to our amateur stations in occupied territory. I got a report from Kansas City. It's about—Diane."

Operator 5's lips tightened. "Dead?" he asked tautly.

Z-7 nudged Tim Donovan. "Tell him quickly, Tim."

"No, Jimmy, she's not dead. She's a prisoner. She was ordered held by von Hauglein when she went to bring him the key. When Hauglein didn't return, somebody at the City Hall recognized her. She was made prisoner and taken to the emperor. Rudolph arranged a fancy execution for you, thinking that you were the Man in the Iron Mask. It was von Hauglein, masked just the way he was when we delivered him to Rudolph's soldiers. Rudolph took the mask off him after he hung him, and found it wasn't you. He became a madman. He had Diane there to witness your execution—but now that his own aide was hung he's going to take it out on her. He's designated a week from tomorrow—the Fourth of July—as a national holiday throughout the Central Empire to celebrate the loss of American independence. And he's going to hang Diane in the Liberty Bell at high noon as the climax of the celebration!"

Jimmy Christopher looked at Tim with suddenly dull eyes. The news that Diane was a prisoner came to him as a body blow at a time when he should have had nothing else on his mind.

For a long heartbeat of time he said nothing, then he turned away abruptly from his good friends there in the small group. Tim Donovan wanted impulsively to comfort him, but Slips McGuire, shrewd little ex-pickpocket, wise in the ways of the world, restrained the lad. "Leave him alone," he whispered. "It's something he's got to fight out by himself!"

Z-7, who had been watching Jimmy Christopher compassionately, nodded, and the three moved away a little, into the
shade of the hotel, and watched the sudden bustle of activity
which Operator 5's quick orders had brought to the town. Men
were scurrying everywhere. Some were trundling the big planes
off the road, out into the field; others were bringing burlap sacks,
tarpaulins, blankets, with which to cover the Sigismunds from
observation from the air; still others were driving up in autos of
every vintage and description which they had commandeered
from garages, back alleys and parking lots. There were fourteen
new, white half-ton trucks upon whose panels was painted the
name of a new ice cream company that had only a short while
ago opened a plant here in Windsor. Little did the officials of
the Windsor Ice Cream Company think, when they ordered
those trucks, that the machines would soon be pressed into a
more glorious service than the delivery of ice cream.

HANK SHERIDAN himself was superintending everything. The machine guns were being moved out of the hotel,
the police station and the garage, loaded onto the trucks. Hank,
exhibiting canny foresight, did not permit the autos to be driven
up too close to the planes, leaving plenty of space on the road
for Z-7's plane to take off. Everywhere there was a new spirit of
hopefulness, almost of happiness. These men were at last seeing
a chance to meet the invader with some of the same medicine
that had been dosed out to their country.

Only in the breast of Operator 5 was there no gladness. Diane
Elliot had come to mean much more to him than he had ever
thought to permit. Through the years this beautiful, gifted girl

had subordinated her own career as a brilliant newspaper woman to the ideal to which Jimmy Christopher was devoting his life. She had been his companion in high adventure, had shared his risks and his triumphs. And the bonds of affection between them were all the stronger because each knew that such affection could never have the normal consummation of marriage until Operator 5 ceased being a number in the service of his country and became once more James Christopher, private citizen.

Now, as Jimmy Christopher stood alone in the center of bustle and activity which he had himself inspired, he felt strangely alone—even though he knew that each of the three who stood on the steps of the hotel, watching him with compassionate gaze, would gladly have sacrificed life itself for his sake.

Jimmy's face was set, sphinx-like, as he suddenly turned and walked toward them. Z-7, standing erect in spite of his broken body, met Operator 5's gaze squarely. "Jimmy," he said clearly, "Tim and Slips and I understand your problem. You are needed very badly here; but if you choose to go to the aid of Diane, it is your right. You have earned it!"

Jimmy said tightly, though there was pain in his eyes: "That is what I'm going to do, Z-7. God help me, I can do no less for Diane. You will have to take charge here, Z-7. You are a better organizer than I am, anyway. You go and take care of getting those anti-aircraft guns rolling and start the recruiting machinery to work. Then come back here, and I'll turn everything over to you. With Tim and Slips to help you—"

Tim Donovan interrupted him, shaking his head violently.

"Nix, Jimmy. I go with you." His chin stuck out defiantly. "And try to stop me!"

Jimmy shrugged. "All right. If the general deserts his post, I guess he can't expect others to stick."

Tim Donovan was suddenly contrite, as he caught the bitterness in Jimmy Christopher's voice. "Gee, Jimmy, don't say that! I—you—you make me feel—aw, gee!" the lad's shoulders sagged. "All right, Jimmy, I'll stay here if you say so."

Jimmy smiled wearily. "I'm sorry, Tim. Forgive me. You can come along. And it won't be exactly desertion. I have an idea in mind."

Tim demanded eagerly: "What is it, Jimmy? A stunt?"

"No, not a stunt. Don't you see," he addressed himself more to Z-7 than to the others, "that no matter how well we fight here, no matter how many of us are willing to die, we can't really stop the armies of the Central Empire in this way? Even when all these bands of men are organized along the entire front of the enemy's advance, they will still be only guerrilla outfits opposed to a modern, highly disciplined, superbly equipped army. We can give them trouble, slow them up, yes. But drive them back, never!"

Z-7 nodded slowly in agreement. "That thought was also in my mind, Jimmy. But it seemed to me that it was better, if the country is doomed to perish, for us to fight every inch rather than to throw in the sponge."

"True. But maybe it's not in the books for this country to be annihilated just yet.

Maybe there's a way to beat Rudolph."

"And that way is?" Z-7's eyes were glittering with taut expectancy.

"Just think," Jimmy went on. "Rudolph now controls all of the United States east of the Mississippi, and for some distance west. In that territory are some sixty or seventy million Americans. Rudolph's entire armed force does not exceed two and a half million. Suppose the sixty-five million were provided with secret leadership; suppose they were welded into a well-knit secret organization, provided with a carefully worked-out plan to seize arms and ammunition; to take possession of strategic points behind the front lines. Suppose that this took place just at the time when you, at this end, had mobilized your greatest strength in manpower and started a determined push. Do you think the two-and-a-half million would be able to stand against us, deprived of their supply bases, attacked from in front and from behind?"

Z-7 nodded. "You've outlined the one and only way in which the Central Empire can be beaten. But it is a thing impossible to accomplish. Rudolph is aware of such a possibility. That is one of the reasons why he has adopted such repressive measures. Anyone who undertook to launch such a movement in the occupied territory would be picked up within twenty-four hours, and beheaded—or worse."

"That," Jimmy Christopher said tightly, "is the chance I'm going to take. I'm going to try to stop Diane's execution; and I'm going to start a revolt in the occupied territory that will kick the props out from under the feet of His Imperial Majesty, Rudolph the First!"

Tim Donovan grinned happily. "Me, too!" he said.

CHAPTER 8
THE FIRST GREAT VICTORY!

O NCE JIMMY CHRISTOPHER had made his decision, he became a veritable dynamo of energy. He saw Z-7 off in the plane, piloted by Tim Donovan, promised Tim that he would wait for the lad to return before starting on the mission into the occupied territory. Then he dragged Hank Sheridan away from the business of getting the autos arranged, got him into the hotel and secured from him a list of the various amateur stations with which communication had been established.

For the next twenty minutes Jimmy Christopher issued whirlwind orders over the radio, consulting maps, choosing spots all over the Dakotas and Nebraska where the isolated bands of Americans were operating, promising to send them guns and recruits as soon as they were available. To all those with whom he talked it was as a new breath of life to learn that Operator 5 was still alive, and in active command. When one of the men from downstairs came up to report that everything was in readiness to start for the pass, Jimmy had already made a rough outline of his plans of defense. He selected two men to remain under Sergeant Geffen at the radio and continue to spread the good word. Geffen grumbled a little at being deprived of a chance at action, but Jimmy pointed out to him that it was important to consolidate all the possible fighting men into a coördinated whole in order to ensure the success of the defense. When Geffen realized the importance of his assignment, he ceased to protest.

Jimmy, in the uniform of a major of the Central Empire, went out with Hank Sheridan and got into the leading car, a beautiful green Cadillac sedan which had belonged to the leading banker of the town. Said banker had left for points west at the first hint of danger, and had taken the train because his chauffeur was in the trenches. Now, that same chauffeur had returned from the front and was driving the same car—but in a different service.

Behind the Cadillac there was a long string of autos, loaded with men and machine guns. The line moved swiftly, negotiated the twenty miles to the pass in fifteen minutes. The road here was wide, having lanes for four cars. On either side of the road was a dry field extending in a gentle slope for about a hundred feet, then rising sharply in a steep ascent. The mountains on both sides of the road formed a natural barrier, impassable to an army without weeks of toil.

Men from the cars swarmed up both slopes, carrying ropes and tackle. Soon, under Jimmy's direction, they were hauling the machine guns up. They had loaded half a dozen bombs from the airplanes into the cars; two of these bombs Jimmy ordered placed along the side of the road, at the mouth of the pass. They were covered with earth, only the detonating caps exposed. Two sharpshooters were stationed at either side of the road, well up on the slopes. Their job would be to explode those bombs by rifle fire at the proper time.

Jimmy, with Hank Sheridan and Slips McGuire at his side,

watched the enthusiastic men hurrying about their work. Then, with a pair of field glasses borrowed from Hank, he climbed up high on the slope and leveled the glasses down at the plain beyond the pass. About ten miles to the east he could see the long, sinuous column of the army of the Central Empire moving forward once more. This time, however, the leading unit was a company of small tanks.

Jimmy smiled grimly. The Central Empire commander was taking no chances on repetition of the strafing that bad taken place earlier in the day. Above the tanks flew the squadron of planes that had pursued Jimmy.

Hank Sheridan, who had climbed up with him, pointed to the planes. "They're stickin' close to the column now," he said, grinning. "They're just waitin' for you to show up again."

Jimmy Christopher nodded somberly, "It's okay now, Hank, but when that column reaches the pass, those planes will fly overhead and drop their loads on the boys here. The anti-aircraft guns can't get here in time, no matter how fast Z-7 works. We've got to figure out some means of checkmating those planes!"

Hank immediately grew sober. "I been thinkin' o' that right along, Operator 5. If we got to die here, I reckon none o' the boys will beef about it—as long as they can do some damage to those skull an' broadsword boys. But I'd hate to have us all blasted out of this place."

Jimmy broke in: "Look here, Hank—how many of your boys can fly a battle plane?"

Hank said uncertainly: "I don't know, but I could find out. Why?"

Jimmy almost pushed him away. "Go on. Find out, Hank, Quick!"

HANK MOVED away, down the slope, calling out to the men as he passed them. Every once in a while one of the men would raise a hand and come to meet him. Sheridan sent the volunteer aviators back to talk to Jimmy while he worked his way down to the path and up the opposite slope. All in all, he sent back more than a dozen men, whom Jimmy talked to. Three of them were youngsters from college who had been taking the recently inaugurated aviation courses that had been introduced on many college campuses. One of them was an ex-airmail pilot, Sam Johnson by name, who had flown the mails for three years; two of them were barnstormers who had toured the country with a flying circus, and who could make planes do handsprings in the air. They were brothers, Joe and Frank Lane, veterans of the World War, who had gone in for barnstorming when they were discharged from the army. Another was a short, squat, swarthy chap named Nick Gatta, who twirled his cap in his hand as he stood before Jimmy, and kept his eyes on the ground.

When his turn came to tell what flying experience he had, he shifted from one foot to the other, and hesitated. "Listen, boss," he finally said. "I can't tell you how come I know how to fly. But you just take my word for it. I can fly rings around any of these other guys. Just give me a plane an' see if I don't tell the truth!"

Jimmy shook his head. "Sorry, Gatta. We only have five planes, and I don't want to lose one of them by turning it over to an inexperienced man. We're going up against that squadron with the advancing army. They're all seasoned flyers, and you've got to be good to stand a chance with them."

The others all perked up their ears. Gatta exclaimed: "Are we really gonna fight them guys in the air? You mean we're gonna take up them crates you captured, and shoot it out with those birds?"

Jimmy nodded. "That's what we're going to do. We have no anti-aircraft guns to protect our boys against attack from the air. So we have to use the planes. And it's mighty important that we succeed, because if we're shot out of the air, the enemy will be able to drop a load of bombs on us that will wipe us out."

Gatta sighed. "Well, boss, I was kinda hoping to keep it a secret. But I'm gonna tell you about myself, because I want a chance at the fun." He lowered his eyes. "The truth is, I been running booze over the border by plane. I done it ever since prohibition started, an' after prohibition was over, I kept it up. There's still a lot of Canadian stuff coming in without paying tax, and I'm the guy that's been bringing a good percentage of it. Sure, it's against the law. But I ain't a bad guy. I'll fight as good as any of them. An' I can work a plane like nobody's business. You gotta be good in my business, or you don't last long!"

He put out a hand pleadingly. "Please! Gimme a chance. Let me once get my hands on those controls, an' I'll stay in the air till I'm blasted down. I'll put up a good scrap!"

Jimmy suddenly nodded. He was thinking of Slips McGuire, to whom he had given a chance in much the same way. And Slips had made good. Why not this man? "You're on, Nick! I'm going to give you one of those planes!"

He left Hank Sheridan in charge of the defense as the select group of pilots, mechanics and observers piled into autos and headed back toward town.

Back in Windsor, Geffen met Jimmy at the door of the hotel. The burly sergeant was beaming. "Tim Donovan sent through word by radio that they landed in Simonton all right, and they've already got a couple of trucks rolling this way with two guns. More coming. And there's a crowd of men at Framington that are preparing to hold the bridge over the Platte, the way you outlined. I told them the next batch of guns goes to them. Word has been coming in from all over that defense units are being organized. Rudolph is going to have no picnic, believe me!"

"Fine!" said Jimmy. "Keep it up!" His men were already trundling the planes out on road, gassing them up. Twenty minutes later, five black planes with the insignia of the Central Empire on their wings, rose into the air over Windsor, and flew east toward the advancing enemy column. But no vicious Central Empire airmen manned the controls of those five engines of destruction. Jimmy Christopher, grim-faced, tight-lipped, flew point in the V-shaped echelon, while Joe and Frank Lane were number two and three respectively on his right and left. Behind the two aerial barnstormers, Sam Johnson, the ex-airmail pilot completed the triangle on the left, while Nick Gatta closed the echelon on the right. Each of the five carried an observer in the rear cockpit and a man in the center pit to operate the bomb mechanism. With the varied and picturesque flying experience of those five—including that of their leader—that particular

136

squadron probably constituted the most dangerous flying unit that had ever taken the air.

From Windsor they rose high, winging eastward, until they passed above Snyder Pass where the three hundred Americans were preparing a warm welcome for the victorious forces of His Imperial Majesty Rudolph I, Emperor of the Central Empire. No single sign down there indicated that the pass was alive with riflemen and machine-gunners. So well had Operator 5 distributed them that their presence could not even be detected by one who knew that they were lying down there in ambush.

THE FIVE planes winged over the pass toward the squadron of enemy ships flying low over the black, creeping tanks that formed the advance guard of the Central Empire army. Each of those tanks resembled an ungainly, huge lumbering beetle, the hideous emblem of the crossed broadswords and the severed head emblazoned in red on the roof between protruding snouts of twin guns which peered out of the metal monsters like wicked, menacing tentacles of death. Behind the tanks marched a whole division of infantry, stretching back as far as the eye could reach.

Above the tanks hovered the enemy squadron, but they had not yet noticed Jimmy Christopher's small air armada, which was intentionally flying high. The first of the tanks was at the mouth of the pass when Jimmy, peering over the side, raised his arm in signal, and lowered it in a swift motion, with finger pointing downward.

Almost as one, the five planes lunged in a mad, screaming power dive straight at the enemy planes. Too late the enemy discovered the doom descending upon them. It is doubtful if even then they realized what was happening, for they saw only a flight of their own ships swooping down toward them. It was only when the five sets of forward machine guns began to spit chattering lead at them that they broke like frightened quail and scurried in frantic haste to escape the hot lead that tore into their wings, that seemed to wrap itself about their struts and to shatter the dashboards before their eyes.

Three of the enemy planes fell in flames under that first devastating attack. Two of them succeeded in evading the long lanes of snarling slugs that whined a song of death about their ears. These two, one of which was piloted by Captain Honig, pulled frantically into a steep climb, with Jimmy Christopher miraculously riding on the tail of Honig's ship. Gatta stuck like a leech to the other. Neither Honig nor his last surviving pilot lasted to the top of their ascent. Both planes crumbled in the air under the stream of bullets from the guns of Jimmy Christopher and Nick Gatta. The deadly air battle was won in the shortest time on record for any multi-plane aerial encounter—one minute and forty seconds. In that short period, five Central Empire crack flyers perished under the guns of their own ships, manned by desperate Americans. And it was the first time since the beginning of the invasion that the Central Empire had been defeated in the air.

Now Jimmy Christopher signaled to his ships to fall into formation once more. Below them he could spot the signs of panic that had swept over the enemy column. The tanks had halted, and their vicious little guns were spitting lead into the air.

Those guns had been designed to serve as land and air offensives, and they now hurled potential death up at the little squadron. But Operator 5 was moving away swiftly, flying—not back over the pass, but forward over the advancing column.

Below them, the marching lines of infantry broke as men fled to the fields on both sides, fearful of bombs. The falling Central Empire planes landed on their own column, and the loads of explosive that they carried burst into geysering destruction among the tanks, shattering them, sending fragments of steel high into the air. The guns of the tanks ceased to snarl. Of the dozen metal creeping monsters, only two remained. At a signal from Jimmy, Sam Johnson left the formation, flew back toward them, and the crews of the two tanks scrambled out and fled, deserting their machines to join the mad flight of the panic-stricken infantrymen in the fields on both sides. All over those fields, frantic officers of the Central Empire threatened, shrieked and cajoled, trying to stop the headlong flight of their men. But those infantrymen knew the loads of destruction carried by the black planes above. They had seen all too often how those planes had flown over towns and villages of America and had dropped tons of death. They had no stomach for a dose of the same. Besides, their morale was shattered by the sight of their own ships, for the second time that day, attacking their own troops. They fled.

Jimmy Christopher raced along the enemy column, peering downward closely. Almost a mile back, he found what he sought—a battery of enemy field guns, being hauled by huge tractors. He signaled behind him, and Joe and Frank Lane

Three of the enemy planes fell in flames under that first devastating attack!

motioned to the men in the center cockpits of their planes. Those men waited until the two planes were directly above the battery to pull the bomb release levers. Two huge bombs hurtled downward upon the luckless battery. They struck with shattering detonations, leaving nothing of those guns but a mass of hot, twisted metal. Back and back over the enemy column they flew, dropping their bombs wherever they sighted artillery. There were no more planes with this column. Evidently the Central Empire expected no resistance from a beaten country whose general staff had abjectly surrendered. They were advancing with only the single squadron of planes. And now that that squadron was destroyed, they were vulnerable from the air. So swiftly had Jimmy struck that the enemy had no time to set up anti-aircraft guns. Jimmy found a battery of those long-muzzled cannons, saw that their crews were frantically moving them into position. But his squadron destroyed that battery, too, with a couple of well-placed bombs. No longer was there any threat from that column to the five desperate adventurers in the air. The entire enemy advance was broken up, fleeing, disbanded. On the road were trucks of ammunition and supplies, motionless, abandoned. Twenty thousand enemy troops were fleeing across fields in a frantic effort to escape destruction. It was a smashing victory for the United States—the first since the invasion. And it was far more than Jimmy Christopher had even dared to hope for.

BEHIND THEM, the shrieking, whooping defenders of the pass rushed out from their concealment and took possession of the two tanks. Others of them gave chase to the fleeing Central Empire troops, while still others raced down the road to take possession of the supply and ordnance trucks which had not been destroyed. Above them hovered the five protecting birds of war.

And Jimmy Christopher's face was turned toward the west, where another black ship was winging its way toward them from the direction of Silverton. He knew that Z-7 and Tim Donovan were in that plane. Here was something substantial that he could turn over to Z-7. When the news of this overwhelming victory was spread over the country, recruits would flock to them. New life would be infused into the blood of the American people. But there were many more columns of the enemy advancing along other roads. And there were hundreds and hundreds of planes which Rudolph could hurl against this little squadron. Other victories would not be bought as cheaply as this one.

Yet it was a beginning.

Jimmy Christopher signaled to his squadron to return. The other men in the five ships were jubilant, wild with elation. But Operator 5 flew back, grim and bleak of eye. He had a journey before him, and in his mind was a picture of Diane Elliot swinging like a pendulum from the knocker of the huge Liberty Bell, her beautiful, fragile body being crushed against the metal sides of the bell.

July the Fourth. A week from tomorrow. He set his lips tightly. He must do more than just stop the execution of Diane Elliot. He must justify his journey by a greater accomplishment; for if he could succeed in organizing a wide uprising in the conquered territory, there was a chance, with the new fighting spirit of the Americans here, that America might once more come into its own. This victory was as nothing to what yet remained to be accomplished....

THE EVENTS of the week following the amazing victory at Snyder Pass need no recapitulation here. Every American schoolboy knows by heart how the backbone of American resistance was suddenly stiffened. Every military textbook details at length how Rudolph, enraged at the incomprehensible defeat of his crack troops, ordered the execution of every commanding officer above the rank of captain who had been with his own unfortunate column, and how he then proceeded to hurl his best troops and his heaviest artillery and his ace flyers against Snyder Pass. And the textbooks tell, too, how Snyder Pass miraculously withstood every assault; how its dogged defenders, reinforced with recruits from everywhere, hurled back massed assaults time after time; how the pass was bombarded at long range for twenty-four hours, until the sides of the mountains themselves crumbled; and how, after that merciless bombardment, a division of Central Empire storm troops advanced to find the pass just as strongly defended as before. Nothing, it seemed, could drive the Americans back from Snyder Pass. And its very name came to symbolize for the defenders everywhere the new spirit of American defense.

"Remember Snyder Pass!" will go down in history with such slogans as *"Remember the Maine,"* and *"Ils ne passeront pas!"*

Wherever there were embattled Americans, that slogan turned the tide of defeat. In the Dakotas and in Nebraska, the troops of Rudolph were suddenly checked by desperate defenders. At Framington, on the River Platte, a force of a thousand

Americans stopped the advance of five divisions of Central Empire troops for three days, while frantic appeals for reinforcements went out by radio all over the country. Individuals and bands of men answered that call from Montana, Wyoming, Colorado, Utah, and from as far west as Oregon. A hundred thousand men poured into the section around Framington to take the place of the already decimated original thousand; and Rudolph's divisions were swamped under, hurled back from the Platte in the second great victory of the war.

In Texas and in New Mexico the Central Empire also encountered the desperate resistance of desperate men pledged to die rather than to retreat. The name of the "Dead Man's Battalion" which had been formed that day at Snyder Pass became a nationwide cry. Men pledged themselves to stand and die rather than give up another inch of ground. And Rudolph met that amazing thing which no general can properly take into consideration in planning a campaign—the thing that cannot be properly defined or explained, but which can be summed up in one word: *Spirit*.

THUNDERING CANNON, searing gases, rending bombs, could destroy men, but could not destroy that intangible thing called spirit. The victory that Operator 5 had accomplished at Snyder Pass had awakened the nation. They would not let Rudolph pass; but at the same time, they lacked the sinews of war with which to push back his armies. It was checkmate—with the Purple Emperor holding more than half of the country. And Rudolph was avenging the checkmating of his armies on the defenseless inhabitants of the occupied territory. His reign of terror became even more gruesome, his cruelties more hideous. Thousands of Americans were tortured, other thousands killed in mass executions. During the week following the Battle of Snyder Pass, the soldiers of the Central Empire were granted absolute license by their emperor to visit every kind of torture, agony and indignity upon the civilian population.

The morning of the Fourth of July was a sorrowful one for the nation, in spite of the fact that the invasion was checked. For physical agony was spread over the land like a dreadful pall. Men died in pain, women in shame. Independence Day was celebrated to the echo of screams of agony.

CHAPTER 9
"DEATH TO THE INVADER!"

IN KANSAS CITY, the morning of the Fourth of July opened dismally. Rain was coming down in torrents, as if the almighty heavens wished to wash from the sight of the universe the blood that drenched the streets of the unfortunate city.

At 8:15 in the morning, a large truck was being driven slowly across the viaduct which spans the mud bottoms between Kansas City, Kansas, and Kansas City, Missouri. This truck had an open body, with tall, slatted sides. Its contents were piled high between the sides, and covered with large tarpaulins. At the wheel sat two men in the uniform of soldiers-of-the-line in the armies of His Imperial Majesty, Rudolph I, Emperor of the Central Empire. These soldiers were unshaven, and their faces and hands were speckled with clotted blood which was manifestly not their own, since they showed no signs of having been wounded. The truck clattered over the viaduct, into the streets of Kansas City, Missouri.

From the crack between the tailboard and the floor of the truck body, blood dripped upon the pavement, leaving a grisly trail of red in its wake, to be diluted by the rain that fell steadily, and washed away eventually into the sewers of the city.

Men and women, peering from behind the drawn shades of their windows at the gloomy truck, crossed themselves and whispered low-toned prayers. For they knew all too well the contents of that truck. Each morning now, for the past week, several similar loads, had passed. Out on the outskirts of the Kansas City, were the mass execution grounds established by the emperor. There, every morning at dawn, thousands of Americans were stood in line across a broad field, two hundred at a time. Facing them were an equal number of Central Empire riflemen. The riflemen were expert marksmen, and it was their business each to select one victim and shoot that victim as many times as possible before he or she died. Some of the marksmen claimed to have placed as many as twenty shots in a victim's body before killing him. It had become a sort of game with the brutal troopers, and in the past week they had improved their skill to such an extent that they could keep their victims squirming and threshing about on the ground for almost an hour while they proceeded methodically, brutally, to place slugs in every non-vital spot of the body. They were allowed an hour with each batch of prisoners. At the end of the hour the still warm bodies would be loaded onto trucks such as this one that rumbled across the viaduct, and brought into Missouri.

Rudolph had devised a particularly fiendish sequel to these mass murders. He permitted his soldiers to bring the bodies in and sell them to the dead person's relatives. Daily, in every quarter of every city in the occupied territory, groups of sorrowing people would congregate about these wagons, offering what little money or other possessions they had been able to scrape together in return for the privilege of carting their loved ones away for decent burial. Each batch of prisoners executed was usually arrested in the same section of town the previous day, so that the soldiers knew just where to go to find buyers for their grisly wares.

The particular truck that crossed the viaduct at 8:15 that morning did not, however, proceed in the usual manner. It rolled by several Central Empire patrols in the city and passed within a stone's throw of Convention Hall, where the huge Liberty Bell still hung from its scaffolding, awaiting its next sacrificial offering at high noon in the person of Diane Elliot. From there the truck proceeded eastward, and finally drove into a narrow thoroughfare known as King Street. It stopped before a garage, and one of the two uniformed soldiers got off, looked carefully up and down the street, then called up to the man at the wheel in surprisingly good English: "Okay, Jimmy, give 'em the horn. The coast is clear!"

The man on the truck nodded, sounded his horn three times, quickly, then twice more. Almost at once the garage doors began to roll open, and the truck drove in. The man on foot followed it, and the doors rolled closed once more.

Within the garage, a surprising sight met the eye. This had once been the terminus for the trucks of the city street cleaning department, and the floor space of the garage covered perhaps thirty thousand square feet. There were no trucks here now, but the place was almost entirely occupied by sweating men crowded closely together. Some of these men were dressed in tattered remnants of United States uniforms. Others wore civilian clothes. They all watched eagerly as the two men proceeded to let down the tailboard of the truck. There was no light in here, and the rain pattered against the doors and roof of the building. The heat was great, the air was close and stifling. Yet none of these men seemed to mind it at all.

The two soldiers of the Central Empire took off their stiff-visored caps, and some one brought them wet rags with which they wiped the blood from their faces and hands. They stood revealed now—Jimmy Christopher was the driver of the truck; the other was Slips McGuire.

A SMALL knot of men gathered about them, asking questions. Jimmy said:

"It went off okay, boys. We got the last load through all right. Take 'em away!"

He and Slips stepped to the back of the truck, pulled off the tarpaulins from the high-piled contents. Close to the back, there were three bullet-riddled bodies, which several of the men helped to remove. Jimmy eyed them solemnly. "Poor chaps," he said. "They were killed by Central Empire troops, but we had to use them to camouflage the rest of the stuff in case anyone looked under the tarps. They served their country, even in death!"

The other contents of the truck were far different. Exclamations of delight came from the closely packed men about the truck as they pulled out dozens and dozens of glistening, oiled sub-machine guns, cases of rifles and grenades. Jimmy and Slips passed the weapons out as fast as they came from the truck.

Slips McGuire said to the men: "Operator 5 and I slugged the watchman at the arsenal, and loaded as much as we could on this truck. It took us most of the night to get it loaded. Then we hid four time bombs in the building. They'll go off at twelve o'clock sharp, and Rudolph won't have any more supplies in Kansas City!"

There were low cheers from the men. Soon all the weapons from the truck had been passed out. Just then, Tim Donovan came pushing through the crowd from the office in the rear. His young, freckled face was alight with excitement, and he was clutching a sheaf of papers in his hand. He gripped Operator 5's sleeve. "Jimmy! Everything's set. I've been on the radio all night. There'll be simultaneous outbreaks in every city in the country. The men are all armed and ready to go. At twelve o'clock sharp they'll shoot the works. And Z-7 and Hank Sheridan are scheduling a big push all along the front at the same time!"

Jimmy said thoughtfully: "You sure the men in the other cities have kept the secret as well as we have here, Tim? Have you instructed them all to take the precautions that I outlined?"

"I have, Jimmy. Of course there's a chance that something has leaked, and that Rudolph will pounce on everybody at once just before the zero hour. But we've done the best we can."

Jimmy Christopher frowned. "It'll be touch and go at the start. We'll know right away if we've been betrayed."

Tim scoffed. "Who would betray us? Any American who did that—"

Operator 5 stopped him. "You forget Redfern. There are others like him. Suppose just one man among the thousands in the various cities should feel, like Redfern, that our best course is to yield to Rudolph. He may delude himself into thinking that he is serving the best interests of the country by helping Rudolph to catch the ringleaders of the revolt, and thus save even more bloodshed."

Slips McGuire pushed in between them. "All the stuff is given out, Jimmy. The men are waiting."

Jimmy Christopher shrugged. "It's in the laps of the gods, Tim," he breathed.

He mounted the platform of the truck, and there, in the half light of the garage, he addressed that vast assemblage. He indulged in no impassioned oratory, but spoke in a matter-of-fact voice.

"Men," he said, "you know what we have to do. Each of you is taking his life in his hands this morning. If we fail, each of you will be dead before the day is over. Our plan is a desperate one, yet by its very desperation it may succeed. Those of you with grenades, hide them about yourselves as best you can, and circulate about the city to the spots I have already assigned to you. At the first stroke of noon, you will hurl the grenades at the buildings that have been marked for destruction. Be sure that those of you who have been assigned to the bridges and the viaduct do not fail. It is important that all approaches into the city be cut off, so that no reinforcements can get here until we have complete control. Those of you who have been assigned to the barracks, I ask, particularly, not to feel any compunction about snuffing out the lives of the soldiers quartered there. If you had been in the execution fields this morning, the way I have, you would have no mercy at all for any one wearing this uniform!"

He ripped the scarlet tunic from him, flung it to the floor.

"Gentlemen, I give you the Fourth of July!"

A low cheer went up from the men, and Jimmy sprang from the truck. "Come on, Tim," he said. "You and I have places to go and things to do!"

At five minutes before high noon, a vast throng filled the streets in front of Convention Hall. In spite of the steady rain, they all stood bareheaded, in compliance with an Imperial edict. From under lowered eyelids some of the crowd cast glances of pure hate at the uniformed soldiers of the emperor who lined the streets, armed with sub-machine guns and bayonets. Others among the people looked compassionately at the beautiful, pale, chestnut-haired girl who stood, manacled, upon the steps of Convention Hall, facing the huge Liberty Bell which was scheduled within the next five minutes to ring out its knell of death upon her broken body.

DIANE ELLIOT stood straight and proud between her guards, chin high, allowing the rain to fall upon her unprotected face. The cold drops formed a small cascade down her cheeks and

152

fell upon her bare, white shoulders. Her blouse had been torn from her body, and a wide iron collar had been fastened around her throat. This collar had a hook attached to it, by which she was to be hung from the knocker-rope of the bell.

Diabolically, Rudolph had conceived the idea of this collar. It was a little too big for her neck, so that it would not strangle her. Her neck would be gradually stretched as she hung, with the bell swinging back and forth against her, and in this way Rudolph expected her to live much longer than if she were strangled by a hempen noose. Thus he could cater to the innate sadism of his nature by prolonging her suffering.

On her feet had been placed a pair of specially constructed shoes with a heavy metal rim around the soles and heels, so that the bell would ring more sharply and clearly as it struck.

Diane's eyes roved over the throng, and she smiled sadly. She was witnessing for the last time the light of day. And it was a bitter day on which to die.

Several courtiers and officers were gathered on the steps, grinning at Diane, eyeing her bare shoulders, and making what they considered witty comments. Rudolph had not yet appeared. He was looking through a window of the building, enjoying the extra minutes of agony to which his victim was being subjected by being exposed thus to the public gaze.

But another person came out on the steps. The dark-haired, fiery-eyed Anita Monfred suddenly appeared, dressed in riding breeches, a tight-fitting bright red jacket and cape; and she was carrying a short riding crop. Just as she stepped out, one of the courtiers, a foppish young snip with a carefully waxed little moustache modeled after the emperor's, made a sardonic remark to a companion, with an eye on Diane's white skin. He said it loud enough to be heard by everyone on the steps. Diane understood a little of the language, and her ears burned, but she still held herself erect, unashamedly.

Anita Monfred, on the other hand, flushed, and swung toward the foppish courtier, who was still smirking at his witticism. "You swine!" she cried, and brought her riding crop smartly across the pallid face behind the waxed moustache. The crack of the whip left a welt across the man's cheek, and he cringed, putting a hand to his face. Again and again Anita rained blows upon him, until he turned and fled, followed by the laughter of those courtiers who had a moment before laughed with him.

Anita Monfred turned away with blazing eyes, unfastened the cape from her own shoulders, and put it around Diane, hooking it in front.

Diane met her eyes, said simply: "Thank you. If you want to do something else for me, shoot me—before they hang me in that bell!"

The Baroness Anita's cheeks were still flushed. She was about to speak when a cold, brittle laugh sounded from the doorway of the hall. She glanced in that direction to see Rudolph, attired in the full regalia of his Imperial rank, watching her amusedly.

"My dear Anita," he said, "that was beautifully done—the way you whipped that chap. You have fire in you today, Anita. You are beautiful!"

Anita took a quick step toward him. "Rudolph! You can't

subject this girl to such a dreadful fate as hanging in the bell. Be merciful. Shoot her—if she must die."

Rudolph's eyes went suddenly cold. "No. That girl is the one person through whom I can strike at the man known as Operator 5. I would give anything to have him here today, to witness this spectacle." He stopped, as a clock somewhere in the city began to toll the hour of twelve. "Take her to the bell. Let us see how her pretty neck stretches!"

"No!" shouted Anita. "You shan't do it. I'll shoot her first!" From under her jacket she produced a small, pearl-handled revolver and leveled it at Diane—who faced her calmly, half-smiling. But before Anita could pull the trigger, Rudolph, snarling like a beast about to be deprived of its prey, sprang upon the baroness, struck down her wrist. The revolver exploded into the ground.

And just then the earth beneath them was shaken by a mighty tremor. An explosion rocked the city, and a gigantic spume of smoke and fire rose into the sky from a point somewhere in the eastern part of town. For a moment they were all deafened. And, as if the blasts had been a signal of some sort, other minor explosions began to be heard from all parts of the town.

Men began to move about in the crowd of hitherto cowed citizens, and machine guns and rifles appeared as if by magic.

From the east the huge spume of smoke spread, darkening the sky. Someone on the steps shouted: "The arsenal, sire! The arsenal has exploded!"

RUDOLPH APPEARED dazed, not understanding what was taking place. But in a moment he grasped the situation.

155

For the men with rifles and machine guns had pushed out of the crowd, and were turning those guns on the Central Empire soldiers. In a second the square before the Convention Hall was a hell of gunfire and sudden death. Gray clad troopers were dropping everywhere, riddled by the sudden hail of lead that swept them.

There were shouts, cries that carried even above the machine gun fire. "Down with the invader! Death to Rudolph! Give him some of his own medicine!"

From out of that throng of amazingly armed civilians, there sprang two figures, those of a man and a boy—Operator 5 and Tim Donovan. Operator 5 shucked the covering from a bundle he had been carrying under his arm, revealing a glittering sub-machine gun. Behind him, Tim Donovan held a revolver, and the two rushed toward the steps of the hall. There stood Diane, Rudolph and Anita Monfred, who was dazedly rising to her feet. The courtiers had already fled.

Rudolph seemed to guess by some sixth sense that this man who was moving inexorably toward him was Operator 5. His face paled with terror, and he turned to flee into the building. Jimmy Christopher stopped on the lowest step, deliberately raised the blunt nose of the sub-machine gun so that its ugly snout pointed directly at the back of the fleeing emperor. Jimmy's feet were planted firmly, his body flexed against the imminent recoil. His eyes were cold, hard, as his finger tautened on the trip of the gun that would hurl leaden death into the body of the man who had caused untold agony to American citizens. There was no mercy in those eyes of his now; he was a grim executioner, and he saw in Rudolph not a man, but a mad dog who deserved no better.

But suddenly Jimmy Christopher uttered a low oath, and held his fire. Another figure had interposed itself between his gun and the fleeing emperor—the slim, svelte figure of the dark-eyed baroness, Anita Monfred!

The baroness spread her arms as a shield, and shouted: "Don't shoot, Operator 5! You owe me a life! I saved that boy—" she pointed at Tim Donovan—"and now I ask for the life of Rudolph! You owe it to me!"

Jimmy Christopher shouted hoarsely: "Out of the way!" He thrust the submachine gun forward. In the split second in which the baroness had shouted that appeal, Rudolph was stepping across the threshold of the hall. His back was still visible, but in a moment he would be gone. What passed through Jimmy Christopher's mind in that moment, he himself will never be able to recall. The baroness was facing him, arms outstretched, eyes shining, as if she were glad to take the leaden slugs from the glittering muzzle. All around them maddened citizens were shouting, screaming, attacking Central Empire soldiers, cutting them down, beating them to the ground.

And the broad back of Rudolph could be reached only through the beautiful body of Anita Monfred!

To this day Jimmy Christopher still thinks that he would have fired that machine gun, that he would deliberately have riddled the baroness in order to reach the Purple Emperor—had it not been for the sudden thrust that knocked the gun aside.

Diane Elliot had stepped quickly down beside him. "Jimmy!"

she pleaded, her voice barely audible above the pandemonium in the street "Jimmy, you can't! She saved Tim—" her voice gained in tempo, took on a quality of rushing panic as she saw the implacable resolution in Operator 5's eyes—"and she tried to save me. You can't—"

She stopped as Jimmy Christopher bitterly lowered the sub-machine gun. It was too late. That momentary delay had given Rudolph the chance for his life. The Emperor's brightly uniformed figure had already disappeared within the doorway of the building.

Anita Monfred knew that she had won. Her lips parted in a smile, and she said to Diane: "Thank you...."

Diane demanded of her: "But why? Why in God's name do you protect him? You are not like him!"

Anita Monfred's lips suddenly lost their smile, and her eyes became dark pools of agony. "Because, God help me, I—love him!"

She leaped backward, startled, as Jimmy Christopher gruffly pushed Diane out of the way. "God, Di, you've let him escape!" he shouted, and sprang up the stairs toward the doorway through which Rudolph had disappeared.

But Anita Monfred, with the quick instinct of a tigress protecting her cubs, flung herself through the doorway, slammed the big oak door in Jimmy's face. A bolt shrieked on the other side as it scraped home, and Operator 5 stood, baffled, on the outside.

He turned, looked at Diane reproachful, but she met his gaze without regret. "You mustn't blame her, Jimmy. She is a woman, and I know how she feels. I would have done as much for you."

"Besides," Tim Donovan broke in at his elbow, "there's no way for Rudolph to escape. The city is ours. If he tries to leave the palace, the mob will surely get him!"

JIMMY SHRUGGED, glanced out over the street. Rifle and machine gun fire was echoing from all corners. Gray-clad bodies lay everywhere. The mob, armed with weapons procured by Jimmy Christopher, was making a clean sweep of Kansas City. "Let's go over to headquarters and get the latest reports," he said.

He pushed through the streets, back toward the garage. Everywhere, the Americans were in complete control. Tim Donovan was prancing about joyfully. "Boy!" he exclaimed. "That's showing him! And Rudolph can't get away. All the bridges have been destroyed, and there's no road out of the city. He'll be caught all right!"

Jimmy Christopher stopped abruptly, looking upward. "No, Tim," he said bitterly. "Rudolph won't be caught!"

Tim and Diane followed his pointing finger. There, winging its way eastward, was a huge plane with a helicopter attachment. Two figures were peering down over the side. And since the machine was yet low, it was easy to recognize Anita Monfred and Rudolph.

Tim exclaimed: "Gee! They had that hidden right near by!"

"On the roof of Convention Hall, no doubt," Jimmy added.

Diane smiled palely. "Let her go, Jimmy. If we are victorious, let us be generous. Let us give her a fighting chance for the man she loves."

In silence they moved through the streets, and finally reached the garage. Men were milling around here, almost hysterical with joy. The city was once more theirs, and reports had come in that the *coups* had been successful in many other cities. Slips McGuire, at the radio, was taking down messages as fast as they came in, from Chicago, New York, Philadelphia, and elsewhere.

He came and shook hands enthusiastically with Diane. Then he told Jimmy: "I just heard from Z-7. They're starting a big push, and—"

HE STOPPED as the radio came to life, left them and put on a pair of headphones. Suddenly he paled, and his hands clenched. He wrote rapidly, then tore the earphones from his head, came running to Operator 5 with the message he had just received.

"Jimmy!" he gasped. "Jimmy! It's a message from Z-7. The American Defense Force is bottled up. A Central Empire Army marched down from Canada, and is taking them from the flank. The Purple troops broke our line of defense. Z-7 and Hank Sheridan are caught between two fires around Snyder Pass. If they're licked, the bottom goes out from under our whole plan!"

For a long minute, Operator 5 made no comment. His eyes sought those of Diane Elliot and Tim Donovan. Diane's face was drawn, gray. Her lips formed words, almost inaudible: "And Rudolph—free!"

Suddenly, the tight-flexed muscles of Jimmy Christopher's jaw seemed to soften. He smiled. "Slips!" he ordered. "Have our plane gassed and brought out on the line. We're flying to Snyder Pass at once!"

Then he took Diane and Tim each by the arm. "Let's go, gang," he said. "We're needed out there—at once. We mayn't win, but we'll give them the toughest battle of their lives!" *

* AUTHOR's NOTE: The foregoing novel has narrated the incidents of the so-called "Second Stage" of the Purple Invasion, as historians are wont to term it. In the next issue the author will deal with the "Third Stage" which lasted for forty-five days from the Fourth of July until the evening of the fateful Eighteenth of August, and which has often been referred to as the "Bloody Forty-five Days." The period between the Fourth of July and the Eighteenth of August is probably the most exciting in American History. The task which faced a disheartened America was a well-nigh impossible one, and the stratagems to which Operator 5 was compelled to resort, the hairbreadth escapes and the moment-to-moment peril of his courageous little band, will make the next novel the most engrossing reading that has ever appeared in the saga of the Purple Invasion.